The Girl In Red

John Nicholl

Also By John Nicholl

The DI Gravel Series
Portraits of The Dead (Book 1)
Before I met Him (Book 2)
A Cold Cold Heart (Book 3)
Anonymity (Book 4)

Dr David Galbraith Series
White is the Coldest Colour (Book 1)
When Evil Calls Your Name (Book 2)

Chapter 1

Kathy Conner stood at the range cooker and stirred the home-made vegetable soup she'd been preparing for over an hour. Had she added salt? Oh God, he always wanted salt. Think, Kathy, think. It *had* to be perfect. Nothing less was acceptable.

Kathy took a spoon and tasted it, ignoring the burning heat as it blistered her lip. Not bad, not bad at all, just the right amount of salt and a little black pepper too. Perhaps he'd be satisfied this time. Maybe it was tasty enough… even for him.

She checked the clock above the dishwasher for the umpteenth time that afternoon and winced. Time was getting on; sprinting away from her faster and faster as if to taunt her. He'd be back soon after five. That only gave her two hours at best. The main course. Come on, Kathy. There are potatoes to peel, vegetables to chop to the correct dimensions. The meal had to be ready and waiting the second he arrived. There was no room for dawdling – not a single second to spare.

Kathy stopped mid-step on approaching the fridge and stood listening for even the slightest sound. Was that a car pulling up on the driveway? What on earth? It couldn't be, could it? It was only ten past three. Oh shit, surely not? Please don't be him. Please don't let it be him.

She noticed that her hands were trembling, her head swimming as she allowed the countertop to support her weight. The driver had switched off the engine. Oh God, was that a key in the lock? Yes, yes, the front door was opening. It was definitely opening. There were footsteps in the hall, heavy footsteps, *his* footsteps, getting nearer. And then there he was in front of her, standing at the kitchen door, flexing his powerful biceps and forming his hands into tight fists as he stared at her with a blank expression on his boyish, brutal face.

'Hello, Michael, you're early today. It's just after three. Have you forgotten something? I'm in the process of preparing your evening meal.'

He glared at her without response, turning his head slowly to scan the room with keen eyes that she believed saw everything.

Kathy looked away, averting her eyes to the wall, wondering why her mouth felt so very dry. 'Did you have a good day at work?'

He took a single step towards her. 'The usual crap. Why do you ask?'

She bit the inside of her cheek hard, tasting blood. 'I'm just taking an interest. That's okay, isn't it? You don't mind, do you? You often say I should.'

He placed his peaked cap on the pine table. 'Can you see this uniform? The dark blue cloth. The shiny silver buttons. Or are you blind as well as stupid?'

Kathy clenched her jaw, continuing to stir the soup slowly with a wooden spoon, avoiding his accusing gaze. 'Of c-course, I can see it. You look very smart. Just like you always do. Your uniform fits perfectly. You're a credit to the force.'

'So you can see it? You're not oblivious to the fact that I'm standing here in full uniform? You're twenty-eight not eight. That reality shouldn't be beyond your feeble capacity for reasoned thought.'

Kathy's entire body was shaking now, her voice breaking as she searched for the words. Any words that may satisfy him even for a single second. Something to calm him down. 'Yes, I can see you. You're right there in front of me.'

'In that case, you should understand that I spend every second of every working day dealing with the criminal lowlifes of this world. The scum that most people choose to avoid. Where's the pleasure in that, Kathy? Can you answer that for me? Or are you just being your usual thoughtless self? Perhaps you're trying to piss me off, is that it? It won't go well for you if you are. Even you should understand that by now.'

Kathy momentarily thought that she couldn't respond; that her mouth wouldn't function; that the words wouldn't come. She forced her lips apart, loosening her jaw, thinking she had no choice but to say something. But what to say? What on earth to say?

'I was only asking. You like me to take an interest, don't you? You've told me as much. Your life is so much more interesting and worthwhile than mine.'

Michael Conner took a second step towards his wife, loving every anxious twitch of her face as he studied her closely.

'You were only asking? Are you sure, Kathy? Are you really sure? Or are you just saying what you think I want to hear? Perhaps you're talking crap as usual. It wouldn't be surprising, now that I think about it. I wonder why I put up with you sometimes. I was quite a catch. I could have married anyone I chose. Why the hell did I settle for a burdensome shrew like you?'

Kathy opened her mouth intending to speak but then closed it again as she choked on her words. Sometimes silence was best. And sometimes nothing helped. She feared this was one of those times.

'Nothing to say for yourself?'

'Nothing you'd want to hear.'

He laughed, head back, and then mimicked her, his mouth hanging open, a half-witted expression transforming his features.

'What's with the goldfish impression? You look even more ridiculous than you usually do, and that's going some. What a fucking idiot! And just when I thought I couldn't like you any less.'

Kathy felt a single tear roll down her cheek. 'I'm sorry, Mike. I didn't mean any offence. That's the last thing I'd want. I'm trying my best, really I am.'

He shoved her aside, staring into the saucepan for a second or two, a look of utter disdain on his face.

'What's this shit?'

Kathy shifted her weight from one foot to the other. 'Um, it's, err... it's vegetable soup. All fresh, all organic. And seasoned just how you like it. Shall I fill you a bowl?'

'Surely you don't expect me to survive on that slop?'

'It's just a starter, that's all. There's Welsh lamb to follow. The very best, and with all the trimmings. All your favourite vegetables and mint sauce too.'

He opened the cooker door, peering in before grabbing her by the hair, dragging her towards him and forcing her head inside the oven, face first.

'Can you see any lamb cooking, Kathy? Take your time. Have a good look around because I couldn't see a fucking thing when I looked. Perhaps I should give work a ring and call in a search team. Maybe a couple of sniffer dogs, huh? Perhaps they could find it. Maybe they'll have more luck than I did. What do you think?'

She was weeping now, her chest tightening as she gasped for breath. 'But y-you arrived home early. I wasn't expecting you for hours. How w-was I supposed to know?'

Michael yanked her back, throwing her to the floor in one powerful movement.

'Or perhaps you'd like to phone them yourself? You like ringing the police, don't you, Kathy?'

'I'm s-sorry.'

He mimicked her for a second time, screwing up his face.

'Oh, please help me, Mr Policeman. My big, bad husband is hitting me again. Blah de, blah de, fucking blah! It was something like that, wasn't it, bitch? When you rang last night. When you dialled 999 and screamed for help.'

Kathy curled up into a tight ball, laying on the kitchen tiles in quivering silence as he loomed over her.

'Have you got any idea how horrendously embarrassing your little drama was for me? I've got to work with those people on a daily basis. That young constable couldn't get out of here quickly enough. He was absolutely crapping himself. Or did you miss that small fact?'

'I'm sorry, I'm truly sorry.'

'You're mentally ill, Kathy. That's what I've told them all. You are round-the-fucking-bend, my cross to bear. And they believe me. They sympathise. They swallow every word I say.'

'I kn-know they do.'

He glared down at her, spitting, snarling; his face strangely distorting.

'Oh you do, do you? Madam knows! Be very careful, bitch. You're playing with fire. Call the police again and you may kill yourself next time. You may take a blade and slash your throat from ear to ear, blood splashed everywhere, with your worthless life draining away to oblivion. Do you understand what I'm saying to you? Do you get my meaning? I could make your death look self-inflicted in the blink of an eye. You were depressed, suicidal with unresolved grief. That's all I'd have to say in explanation at any inquest. Your death would be of no consequence to me or anybody else, none at all. If you want to know something, know that. You may live a little longer if you do.'

'I'm s-sorry. I shouldn't have rung. I realise that now. I r-really shouldn't have rung.'

Michael rested his boot on the side of her head, pressing down.

'No, you shouldn't have. And you won't do it again, will you, bitch? Not even you'd be that stupid. Because no one is ever going to listen to you. They're never going to listen to anything you say. And then you'd pay the ultimate price.'

'No.'

He increased the pressure, agitating his foot to and fro as if grinding a discarded fag butt into the gutter. 'No what, Kathy? No fucking what? Spell it out, bitch. Plead your case.'

'No, I w-won't ring again.'

'Are you sure?'

'Yes, I'm sure.'

'Repeat yourself. I couldn't hear you through all that pathetic snivelling.'

Kathy repeated herself – louder this time – and hated herself for it.

'Now that was much better. A lesson learnt. No one's ever going to help you. Not the police, not your mother and not that moronic twin sister of yours. Because they all think you're totally bonkers, as crazy as a bag of monkeys, loop the fucking loop. No one's ever going to take anything you say seriously. Not for a single second. They've got their own lives to worry about. They don't give a flying fuck about you and your issues. And if you try to leave again, I'll find you. I'll bring you back. Just like last time. Just like every time. And then you'll suffer. You'll really suffer. You'll pay a heavy price for the inconvenience and irritation you've caused. You're mine, Kathy. I own you. You're my property to do whatever the hell I like with. Do you get it? Has it finally sunk into that thick head of yours? You're less than human. You don't have the same rights as real people.'

'I'm s-sorry.'

'Repeat it.'

'I'm sorry.'

'Louder!'

'I'm sorry!'

He held the sole of his boot to her mouth. 'Lick it.'

'What?'

'Just lick the fucking thing like the bitch you are.'

Kathy slowly stuck out her tongue. She inched it closer and then began to rub the tip of it against the sole of his boot. She gagged, but then licked some more out of fear of the boot coming crashing down on to her mouth. Eventually, Michael pulled his foot away. He shifted towards the cooker, lifting the heavy saucepan, then dribbling hot soup over her legs before strolling casually around the kitchen and pouring it over the floor and various work surfaces.

'Oh dear, now look what you've made me do, you stupid bitch. Useless, that's what you are. You're a mess, Kathy. I don't know why I put up with you. You're a fucking disgrace.'

The bastard, the absolute bastard! 'I'm s-sorry. I'll try to do better. I promise I'll do better.'

Michael threw the saucepan to the floor. 'What good does *sorry* do you? No fucking good at all, that's what! You need to up your game, lady. Maybe then I wouldn't have to punish you quite so often. Perhaps then you wouldn't drive me around the fucking bend with every breath you take.'

Kathy cringed, clutching her knees to her chest as he returned to her side. One day she'd escape the bastard. One day she'd get away.

'I'll do better. I promise I'll d-do better.'

He shook his head dismissively.

'Oh yeah, that will be the day, little Kathy Conner performing her meagre responsibilities to an acceptable standard for once in her sad life. I've heard it all before, more times than I care to remember. You're useless, woman. There's more chance of you flying around the room like the witch you are.'

Kathy glanced up with sad, heavy eyes and then quickly looked away, the fine hairs on her arms standing to attention, pressing against her sleeves. It seemed he'd had enough. He was losing interest. Thank God for small mercies.

'I'll try harder. I promise I'll try harder.'

'I'm heading back to work now to spend some time with people who matter. People who do something worthwhile with their lives, as I do. I strongly suggest you make certain that this place is utterly spotless by the time I get back. No shortcuts, no cutting corners, totally immaculate, not a hint of dust. Let's see if you can actually live up to your promises for a change. Or are you full of crap as per usual?'

Just go. Please go and never come back.

'I'll do m-my very best.'

'I'll be checking, make no mistake. I'll be making a full inspection, every corner, every crevice, so I suggest you try to get it right for once. Come on, don't just lay there lingering like a bad smell. You need to get on with it. Get on your feet. The clock's ticking!'

'I'll start s-straight away. As s-soon as you've gone through the door.'

He smirked sardonically. 'And you'll do your best? Just like you said. As you promised.'

'Yes, absolutely, I'll clean every inch of the room to the very best of my ability.'

He picked up his cap, tossed it in the air, caught it casually, walked towards the hall, then called out without looking back.

'Oh, I'm sure you will, Kathy. But the problem is, your best is never good enough. It never was, and it never will be.'

Chapter 2

Inspector Michael Conner looked up and smiled as Detective Sergeant Sarah Hodgson approached his table with a cup of freshly brewed tea in one hand and a bacon roll in the other.

'All right, Sarah, long time no see.'

She sat opposite him, picking up a bottle of brown sauce.

'Yeah, I haven't been based here for very long. So I thought, what the hell, why not take full advantage of the canteen now that I've got the opportunity?'

Conner sipped his drink, smiling for a second time, revealing even white teeth that shone.

'So, how's life treating you? Someone mentioned that you've got engaged. Who's the lucky guy?'

Hodgson reached out her ring hand with a grin, enjoying the attention. 'Jonathan Sharp, Jon Boy, you must know him, he's a DC in the Charles Cross area.'

Conner nodded his recognition.

'Ah, yes, of course I do. Nice bloke, we trained together years back.'

She took a bite of the roll and nodded.

'Oh yeah, I remember Jon saying something now that you mention it. He's planning to get in touch before the stag night if you fancy it?'

'Sounds good to me.'

'You can keep an eye on him for me. Make sure he comes back in one piece.'

Conner slurped his coffee and laughed.

'Good luck with that, the lads tend to make the most of it when they get together for a celebration. He may well end up handcuffed to a lamp post with his trousers and pants around his ankles.'

'I hope they don't go over the top, that's all.'

'So, when's the big day?'

'January fifth, in Cuba! It was Jon's idea. And his mum and dad are paying for it all, God bless them. There are fifteen of us going over together from Gatwick. Just family and a few close friends. It looks like a beautiful place from what I've seen online. I can't wait. It's going to be brilliant.'

'It all sounds wonderful. I wish you every happiness. You both deserve it.'

She paused before responding.

'How's Kathy, Mike? I heard things aren't so great.'

He removed a clean white cotton hankie from a trouser pocket, dabbing at each of his eyes in turn as they reddened and filled with tears.

'So, what did you hear?'

'That she's been making wild allegations again.'

Michael dropped his head, focussing on the tabletop to avoid her gaze.

'It's been absolutely horrendous, to be honest. I don't know what to do for the best. Kathy's been on antidepressants for months, but they don't seem to be helping in the slightest. She's never been the same since losing the baby last year, that's the truth of it. It hit us both so very hard, but Kathy just can't come to terms with our loss. It's as if it happened yesterday. She was so very happy when she found out she was pregnant, making plans, decorating the baby's bedroom, choosing names, buying the cot and everything that goes with it. But then a few weeks later the baby was gone, as if he'd never existed in the first place. Life can be so very cruel.'

'You knew it was going to be a boy?'

'Yes, after a scan, we were planning to call him Robert after Kathy's late father.'

Hodgson swallowed hard. 'I'm so very sorry.'

'It was a truly awful time for both of us. All that hope, the anticipation, coming to such a tragic and sudden end. Kathy fell apart. She totally disintegrated. I tried to help, I tried to support her, but nothing I ever said or did made even the slightest difference. After five happy years of marriage that one awful event wrecked our lives. Kathy didn't stop crying for days, and then when I thought things couldn't get any worse, the depression *really* set in. She'd just sit there, staring into space with a blank expression on her face for hour after hour. She thought she heard the baby crying one awful night I'll never forget. She stood in the bedroom, shaking me awake and saying she'd heard the unmistakable sound of a small child whimpering. She rushed around every room in the house, upstairs, downstairs, looking in every cupboard and drawer while I desperately tried to persuade her to see sense. She collapsed to the kitchen floor in the end, weeping uncontrollably as her chest heaved and she gasped for breath. I'd never seen anyone in such a state. Not even on the job.'

'That's terrible, Mike, I can't think of anything worse.'

'I think Kathy blames me in some strange way she can't even begin to explain. As if the baby's death was *my* fault. As if I could have waved a magic wand and prevented the miscarriage. If only life were that simple! I've tried telling her things can get better with time. But she doesn't want to hear it. She's turned against me. It's not possible to reason with her anymore.'

Hodgson blew the air from her mouth for a full two seconds, carefully considering her choice of words.

'My sister had postnatal depression after her second one. Completely out of the blue. It was bad. I know it's not the same as what the two of you are going through, but she's over it now. That's what I'm trying to get at. Hopefully, Kathy will pick up soon too, just like my sister did. I always liked Kathy. I hate to think of her as unhappy as she so obviously is.'

His eyes narrowed. 'Are you saying you know her?'

'Well, yeah, or at least I did when we were teenagers. We went to the same church youth club. We were good mates for a time.

Plymouth is a relatively small pond. Most people know each other in one way or another.'

'She never said anything.'

'Why would she? We were kids. It was years ago. We haven't seen each other for ages.'

Conner acknowledged Sarah's observation with a subtle nod of his head, trying to read her thoughts, to drive home his advantage.

'Kathy's psychiatrist said she's going through a grieving process of sorts. He explained it to me – man to man – when she was out of earshot. She's stuck at the anger stage, that's what he said. I get it, I do – but why she has to take it out on me time and again I don't know. It seems never-ending. I still love her, she's still my Kath, but she's changed beyond all recognition. Life's blunted her edges and warped her thinking. It's taken a heavy toll.'

Hodgson screwed up her face. 'I didn't realise things were quite as bad as they seem to be.'

'We were close once. Really close. Kathy's the love of my life, my soulmate, but I can't take much more. She's breaking my heart one day at a time. I try to focus on work, to look for the positives, but it's getting harder with every day that passes. I'll be on the happy pills myself soon if the situation doesn't change. She tells so many lies. To me, to anyone who's willing to listen. Horrible lies, cruel lies. She tries to hurt.'

'I'm so sorry; I don't know what more I can say.'

'It's truly unbearable at times. If someone had told me how bad things would get, I wouldn't have believed them.'

Hodgson forced out an unconvincing smile which quickly faded, a small part of her wishing she'd sat talking to somebody else entirely.

'I guess Kathy's hitting out and you're in the firing line. You're an easy target. That's how it happens sometimes. People hurt those who are closest. You should have heard some of the things my sister said to me when she was at her lowest. Hang on in there, Mike, that's my advice. Things will pick up sooner or later. Everything passes, it's just a matter of time. My sister is happy again now.

They've had another child and life's looking rosy. It's almost as if her depression never happened.'

Conner wiped a tear from his cheek, meeting her eyes, holding her gaze until she looked away.

'I bloody well hope so, Sarah. She's even talked of suicide. An overdose, slashing her wrists, hanging herself by the neck, the list goes on and on. I'm worried sick every time I leave her alone in the house. The girl still means everything to me, even with all her problems. It would break my heart if she followed through on her threats. I imagine myself walking in from work one day and finding her dead. The possibility haunts me, but what can I do? I can't watch her every second of every day. Not unless I set spy cameras up in the house. I only wish I could.'

Hodgson reached across the table and patted his hand. 'Things will get better. They'll work out in the end. Just like I said. You wait and see.'

'I hope so, Sarah. I really hope so. Life's like a waking nightmare at times. I don't know how much more I can take.'

Chapter 3

Kathy was still cleaning a spotless kitchen floor when her husband returned to the house at just gone seven o'clock that evening. She tensed as he strolled casually around her, carefully examining every inch of the room with cold eyes, seemingly devoid of emotion.

'Hello, Mike. I'm nearly done. Is there anything I can get you? How about a nice cold beer and a slice of melon before I dish up your meal? I've got a particularly sweet and juicy golden honeydew in the fridge. I could serve it with a little brown sugar, just as you like it. And with a glacé cherry on top. You'd enjoy that, wouldn't you? You usually like cherries.'

Kathy felt his hot alcohol-soaked breath on her skin. The stink of it filled her nostrils as he stood behind her, hissing into her ear at touching distance.

'Why the fuck didn't you finish cleaning this place before I got home? It's been hours since I went back to work. Are you really that inept? I made my expectations perfectly clear in simple language even you should have been able to understand. Clean the place. That's all I told you. Clean it properly before I arrive home for the inspection. Surely, even you should have been able to finish in time for my arrival. That's not too much to ask, is it? Can't you even manage the simplest of tasks to a basic standard? A trained chimp could manage as much. Why so pathetically slow?'

Kathy dry gagged, swallowed, and gagged again as she searched for the right words. Anything to appease him. Anything to bring the interaction to an end, whatever the outcome.

'I wanted to m-make sure everything was perfect for you. Cleanliness is next to godliness. It's my purpose in life. That's what you said, wasn't it? I was simply following your instructions, that's all. I'm sorry if I've let you down again. I didn't mean to. I just wanted it to be perfect. I'll try to do better next time.'

He grabbed her ponytail, jolting her head back sharply and holding it there for a few seconds before speaking again.

'Nothing you do is *ever* perfect, bitch. Not even close. You're a fuck up. A lower form of life, a slug, a rodent, a waste of space and oxygen. You should know that by now. I've told you often enough. Weren't you listening? Perhaps you should clean out your ears. Hitler had the right idea. If I put you out of your misery, it would be a service to humanity.'

'I'm doing my b-best, Mike. Honestly, I am! Why don't you sit yourself down in the lounge and I'll get you that cold beer I mentioned? I think there's a football match on the BBC. You like football, don't you? You could sit back and relax after a hard day. That would be nice, wouldn't it? I could serve your food one course at a time whenever you're ready. You could ring the bell or shout out, and I'd come running.'

Michael drew his leg back and kicked Kathy's blue plastic bucket hard, sending a stream of warm and soapy water spilling across the floor from one end of the kitchen to the other.

'Are you trying to get rid of me, Kathy? Is that what you're doing with your offers of beer and food and sport? Is that your little game? Do you really think I'm that stupid? I hope not, for your sake. That wouldn't go well for you. It wouldn't go well at all.'

'Of course I'm n-not trying to be manipulative. I'm just trying to be nice, that's all. I'm trying to be a good wife. The kind of wife you deserve. I'd never underestimate you, not for a single second. I know you're much cleverer than me. I'd never suggest otherwise. You're the master and I'm the servant.'

'You're never going to get rid of me, bitch. I own you. Not that you're worth very much. I wonder why I waste my time on you sometimes. Maybe I should sell you. That's assuming anyone would be willing to pay.'

Kathy looked away, focussing on nothing in particular.

'I just t-thought you'd enjoy a nice snack. I didn't mean anything b-by it. I want to make you happy. I like to see a smile on your face.'

He lurched forwards, grabbing her forearm tightly, digging his nails into her soft flesh, rushing her towards the hall.

'Best not try to think for yourself, there's a good girl. Just follow my orders, if you can manage that much without yet another cock-up. I think that's advisable, don't you? Leave the thinking to those of us with a fully functioning brain, eh. You'd only make a fool of yourself again like you always do.'

'I'm sorry.'

'You amaze me sometimes. Why embarrass yourself? Are there any lows to which you won't stoop?'

Kathy stumbled, losing her footing as he dragged her towards the staircase in the hall.

'You can't even walk in a straight line without falling over. It would be funny if it weren't so pathetic. What the hell is wrong with you, woman? Is there nothing you can do without fucking up?'

Kathy lifted herself to her feet with the aid of the bannister, wincing as she felt a thin stream of warm urine running down one leg, soaking into her jeans. 'Sorry, Mike, I didn't mean to offend.'

'You never fail to let me down.'

'I don't know w-what more I can say.'

'Stop your pathetic snivelling, woman. What use are apologies? Now get up those stairs, take a hot shower, brush your teeth, apply some perfume to mask your stink, and lie face down on the bed until I get there.'

She ascended the first two steps on trembling legs, not looking back, never looking back, praying he'd disappear, wishing she'd never met him in the first place.

'Would you like me to wear any particular perfume for you?'

'Why do you always feel the need to ask? Aren't you capable of even the most basic decision without my input? It's perfume, not rocket science.'

Kathy whispered her words just about loud enough to make herself heard.

'I w-want to be sure I choose the right one, that's all. I wore the wrong one last time. It made you angry. You punished me. You didn't like it at all.'

He sighed theatrically, forcing the air from his mouth.

'Wear the one my mother sent you last Christmas, the one that smells of roses. And use plenty of it. Splash it on. Bath in the stuff if you have to. But, whatever you do, make sure you mask your smell. It's off-putting! You're like a fucking skunk.'

Kathy stood on the landing, statue-like, temporarily unable to move as she searched for the right words to shut him up. But what could she say in the light of such wanton cruelty? Nothing she could utter would engender anything but rage. It was sometimes better to say nothing at all.

'Didn't you hear what I told you, bitch? Am I not speaking English? Or perhaps I'm not speaking loudly enough for you? Please don't tell me that your ears are becoming as useless as the rest of you.'

'I'll wear the perfume as you said. I've plenty left. I'll dab it all over.'

'So, you'll follow orders?'

'Yes, I'll follow orders.'

'And I'm assuming you'll shut the fuck up until I'm done this time. I don't want to hear from you, and I don't want to see your ugly face. You lie there on your belly with your legs open and your fat arse sticking in the air for as long as required. Have you got that into your thick head?'

He stalled for a few seconds, chuckling to himself as he pictured the scene.

'Surely, you can manage that much? Even animals seem to fuck without too much difficulty.'

Kathy wept silent tears as she slowly approached the bathroom door.

'All right, Mike, I hear you. Is there anything else I can do for you? Anything at all? All you have to do is ask. Your wish is my command. I'm here to serve.'

'No, I think that's enough for you to be getting on with. I don't want to overburden your enfeebled mind. What would that achieve?'

'I'll get on with it then, shall I?'

'You do that… And stop all the moronic whimpering before I shut you up for good. What the hell's wrong with you, woman?'

'Nothing, nothing's wrong with me.'

He checked his watch.

'You've got exactly ten minutes to get yourself ready, and then I'll be up. It would not be a good idea to disappoint me again. If I can't get hard, it will be down to you.'

'Okay, Mike. I'll get started.'

'Oh, and one last thing before I let you go. Make sure you piss off back downstairs when I'm finished. You can sleep on the lounge floor. I want the bed to myself. I've got a busy day tomorrow. I want to be at my best.'

Should she ask? Maybe it was worth the risk, yes… no… yes… no?

'What a-about the settee? I slept on the settee last night. Would that be okay? I wouldn't bother you before morning. I could have your breakfast ready and waiting at whatever time suits you best.'

He was snarling now, as angry as she'd ever seen him as he rushed after her two steps at a time.

'Are you deaf as well as stupid? If I'd meant the fucking settee, I'd have said the fucking settee. The floor's good enough for the likes of you! You're lucky you're not sleeping in the shed with the rest of the rats. Even that's better than you deserve. You're probably related to most of them.'

'I'm s-sorry, Mike, I wasn't thinking.'

Kathy lost her footing, dropping heavily to the floor, grazing her left knee. He reached down, grabbed her hair, dragged her to her feet and shoved her towards the bedroom door with one hand while undoing his trousers with the other.

He loomed over her, hateful, radiating spite.

'Now get your knickers off and perch on your knees with your pussy on offer. I've decided not to bother waiting.'

Kathy hesitated, just for a fraction of a second. Fear feeding her indecision as it had many times before.

He knocked her with his foot.

'Too slow, bitch. You're too fucking slow!'

'Have you... have you got a condom?'

'No, I fucking well haven't.'

'But you need to use–'

He punched her hard in the back of her head, twice – making her giddy as she lurched forwards.

'*Please*, Mike, I'm *begging* you. Please use–'

'You can shove your fucking condom. Now, come on, move! I haven't got all day. And make sure you're nice and wet this time. I want to slip in easy. Come on, on all fours, arse in the air. Do it, now! You should be thanking me, not making me wait. I'm man enough for any woman and more than enough for you.'

Chapter 4

Kathy peered out from behind the lounge curtains as a local supermarket delivery van plastered with brightly coloured advertising logos pulled up outside the house she shared with her husband. She checked her watch, rechecked it, and was already waiting in the open doorway by the time her middle-aged delivery man waddled down the path a minute or two later.

'All right, love, you're a keen one today. Put a smile on that pretty face of yours. It may never happen.'

Kathy mumbled her response, barely audible, speaking as much to herself as him.

'Maybe it already has.'

He smiled unconvincingly.

'Where do you want them, love? I'd better get a move on. I've got to be back at the store by two o'clock at the latest. It's all go in this job. No rest for the wicked, eh?'

Kathy nodded once, standing aside to allow him to wobble past.

'Put everything in the kitchen, please. I'll start unpacking while you get the rest.'

He smiled again, spontaneously this time.

'Okay, anything to please. I wouldn't want to see you carrying them yourself. It's all part of the service.'

He carried the groceries from the hall, through the dining room and into the kitchen where he left them on the red-tiled floor before returning to the van to collect the remainder of Kathy's order.

'There you go, love, that's the lot for today. Can you sign this for me? I don't know why. Nobody ever looks at the damn thing.'

'Any changes?'

'No, nothing today, it's all with you as ordered.'

Kathy's relief was almost tangible as she lifted the last of the overburdened grocery bags from their green plastic containers. She stood and smiled before signing the small screen with an unreadable squiggle.

'Thanks again, it's appreciated as always.'

He picked up the two empty receptacles, approached the front door, then turned his head back.

'Are you all right, love? You don't seem yourself today if you don't mind me saying so. There's a bug doing the rounds.'

Kathy raised a hand to her face, masking her eyes for a beat.

'It's nothing. I'm fine.'

'If you say so, love. You look as if you're a bit under the weather to me. My sister had the flu a week or two back. You better look after yourself. You don't want to be in the state she was in.'

He tapped his bulbous nose knowingly with the index finger of his free hand.

'Believe me. I know the signs.'

'I said I'm fine.'

He nodded twice, seeming less than persuaded.

'Okay, if you say so. I'm off next week, so it'll probably be the week after when I see you again. I'm off to Majorca with the missus and the kids for a bit of sun… all-inclusive. It's cheaper at the time of year as long as you avoid the half-term holidays.'

'I really do have to go now. My husband's tea's not going to cook itself. I need to get on.'

The delivery man retreated from the doorstep, squinting as the pale autumn sun caught his face. 'All right, love. I was only making conversation, that's all. Sorry to keep you.'

Kathy shut the door without response, hurrying in the direction of the kitchen, deep in contemplative thought as her gut twisted and complained. Periods didn't stop without good reason. That's what she told herself. That's what she yelled inside her head. She just had to know the truth. One way or the other – pregnant or not – she had to understand the reality, whatever the risks, whatever the danger. She had to comprehend whatever she was dealing with. Nothing was nearly as necessary, and nothing mattered more. It was as simple as that.

Kathy delved into the first carrier bag with urgent, fast-moving fingers, then into another, and then another before finally finding what she was looking for in the fourth. She clutched the white cardboard box tightly in one hand and stared at it, panting hard as her chest tightened and her breathing became more laboured. Come on, Kathy, you can do it, girl, deep breaths. Inaction wasn't an option. Not now, not anymore, she just had to get it done. Maybe her situation had changed forever. Perhaps this was it – the moment that changed everything.

Kathy ran towards the staircase, ascending two steps at a time, despite both vaginal and rectal bruising screaming for attention with each painful step. Please, God, no, not a child, not with him, anyone but *him*! She couldn't go through it again, not again – not after the last time. Grieving one baby was more than enough for one lifetime. What if he did the same awful thing again? And he would if given a chance. He definitely would!

She sat on the bathroom floor, cross-legged, staring wide-eyed as two blue lines appeared in the small plastic window. Oh God, no, it was happening, it was really happening. Why her? Why now? He'd raped her once. Just once without protection! What were the chances? Was God looking down at her and laughing? Or was the devil pulling the strings?

Kathy rose to her feet, refastened her blue jeans, washed her hands with warm, soapy water and returned to the kitchen with her thoughts tumbling. She had to focus. There were things to do – things she had to get right. He couldn't know. He could never know. A child wasn't a part of his plans. He'd left her in no doubt on that score. He'd punch her, kick her, do whatever it took. And he'd blame her for it too when he'd done his worst. That's the sort of man he was. The unborn baby wouldn't stand a chance. He or she'd be dead and gone before ever drawing the breath of life. There would be no celebration, only grief and painful memory.

Kathy pulled on a thick sky-blue woollen cardigan against the unseasonal chill and stepped out into the back garden unsupervised for the first time in almost three years. If she were quick, maybe no one would see her. Perhaps no one would tell him she'd broken his rules. Maybe she'd get away with it without the need for explanation, pleading or punishment. Come on, Kathy, be brave, girl. You can do it. Do it for your baby. Do it for your child.

Kathy repeatedly glanced at the windows of overlooking houses; up, down, right to left and then back again, searching for any sign of non-existent prying eyes, anyone who may speak to her husband, anyone who may give her up and condemn her. She moved quickly now, urging herself on, opening the shed door and looking in. Where is it? Where on earth is it? Oh, thanks be to God! Behind the lawnmower.

Kathy stepped over a pile of half-empty paint tins, careful not to move anything even slightly. If she left any clue, he'd spot it. Just like always. He always spotted even the smallest flaw. She had to be careful. More cautious than she'd ever been in her life. So much depended on her efforts. For her, for the baby, she had to get everything right. Nothing less was acceptable.

Kathy brought her thought process to a sudden end as she took a shovel in one hand, her heart pounding in her throat as if trying to escape her body. She could hear the incessant beat like a distant drum as she approached a flowerbed at the far side of the lawn one considered step at a time, and proceeded to dig frantically, sinking the spade's blade into the cold, dark earth time and again until she finally judged the hole to be of sufficient depth for her purpose. It was big enough, wasn't it? Surely it was deep enough. He wasn't a gardener. He didn't bother with the flowerbeds, and particularly not in autumn when nothing grew, except his self-importance. There were no weeds to pull – no roses to spray. Surely, not even he would find evidence of her activities. I'm doing right thing, aren't I? Course I am. She repeated it in her head, still unconvinced but keen to continue. She had no choice.

Kathy felt her body shudder as she dropped the white plastic tester and its cardboard packaging into the hole. She looked down, experiencing a sudden surge of almost overwhelming panic when they contrasted dramatically against the pitch-dark earth. If he dug there, he'd spot them. He'd definitely spot them. How could he not? They stood out as if highlighted by a spotlight, big, bright and screaming for attention. But why would he dig? He wouldn't, would he? She just had to trust her own judgement. She'd come up with a plan. There was no going back, not now. It was far too late for that. She had to follow it through.

Kathy reached down stiffly, placing the offending items to one side before digging down another two feet or so in a further hopeless attempt to alleviate her angst. There, that's it. Much better. Why would he ever choose to dig that far down? Even if he did do some gardening, which seemed unlikely, it had to be deep enough, didn't it? Come on, Kathy, it just had to be, he'd be back soon, time's getting on. Make a decision and stick to it.

Kathy was panting hard now, her chest rising and falling at a rapid rate as she dropped the items into the hole for the second time. She placed a large, suitably sized stone directly on top of them and pressed it down with the sole of her shoe before shovelling the dark earth back into place, carefully examining it for a few seconds with almost forensic precision. *Not good enough, not nearly good enough!* She heard him yell it in her mind as if to mock her, louder and louder. It had to be as near to perfect as feasibly possible. She couldn't leave even the slightest hint for him to find. He'd been a detective, and a good one, too, according to him. He'd said it and said it; driven it home, never to be forgotten. His return to uniform had been an abomination, a waste of his God-given talents – a decision made by morons. That's what he'd claimed. There was nothing he couldn't find out.

Kathy rechecked her watch, asking herself why the second hand was moving so very quickly, seconds seemingly becoming minutes in the blink of an eye. She curled her toes, dropped onto all fours and began studying the ground carefully, adjusting the position of the surface earth with her fingers until it blended almost precisely with the rest. She repeated the process once, then twice, telling herself that she'd done all she could. She'd done her best; paid close attention to detail. Now, all she could do was put the shovel back exactly where she'd found it, prepare for his return and make like she'd done nothing at all. He'd be back soon enough, with all that entailed. There was no room for dawdling – no time for delay. The clock was ticking. She had to get on.

Kathy took her shoes off before entering the house with the intention of cleaning them, but then it dawned on her, the receipt! Oh God, what if he saw the receipt? It had happened before. He'd sometimes checked what she'd bought. Examined the details with his criticisms, snide comments and worse. Why not this time? It could happen. It really could. She had to find the damned thing and send it to oblivion.

Kathy delved into one plastic bag after another, sweating profusely by the time she finally found the required strip of paper and ripped it into what seemed a thousand tiny pieces. She gathered up each and every speck, double checking that she hadn't missed even one, before running for the stairs, clutching them tightly in cupped hands that wouldn't stop trembling. The toilet, that made sense. Flush the evidence down the toilet. Surely not even he could find them there? Not in the sewerage system, not if she kept her mouth tight shut. Not if she stayed strong and didn't buckle under whatever pressure he imposed.

She dropped all the pieces of paper into the porcelain bowl, flushing once and then again for a second time when one piece floated to the surface, lingering in the water as if to spite her. Kathy stared into the bowl, resisting the impulse to vomit. What if she'd missed it? What if he'd spotted it? She'd had a lucky break. Maybe things were looking up at last. Perhaps fate was on her side this time. The universe conspiring to protect the new life inside her womb. Yes, that made sense. Come on, Kathy, you can do it, girl. Deep breaths, one step at a time. All she had to do was have a super quick shower, apply his favourite perfume, clean her dirty clothes and shoes, dry them, put them back on again and then start cooking his tea. She could manage that much, couldn't she? If she hurried, if she didn't waste a single second. There would be criticisms; there were always criticisms of one thing or another, whatever she did, whatever she said in her defence. But so be it, she'd triumph in the end. Keep saying it, Kathy. Say it and believe it. She had to focus on the end game whatever the cost. Stick to her plan.

Kathy stripped off, stepped into the shower, switched it on, taking fleeting sensual pleasure in the flowing water warming her skin. She could do it and she could win, whatever he said to the contrary. She couldn't let herself become overwhelmed by fear or distress as she had so many times before, frozen by indecision at the hands of her tormentor. Failure was utterly unthinkable now. Everything about her had to be just as it was when he'd left that morning. Nothing to raise suspicion. Nothing to spark his attention or concern even slightly. Attention to detail. That's why she'd failed before. This time had to be different. There were two lives at stake now. There wasn't just her to think about. Another baby wasn't going to die. Not if she had anything to do with it. This time she had to get it right.

Chapter 5

The phone seemed to ring for an age before Kathy finally heard her mother's familiar musical West Country tones.

'Hello, Mum, it's Kathy. I'm glad to catch you in. Have you got time to talk?'

She sighed theatrically before responding, making zero effort to hide her displeasure.

'I was just about to take a nice hot bath with a glass of wine. Can't it wait? I'm your mother, not an agony aunt.'

Kathy swayed from one foot to the other, oblivious to her repetitive movements as her mother's disinterest stung and festered. Should she put the phone down? Was it even worth continuing? Perhaps Mother would take her seriously this time. Maybe she'd even believe her for once in her life.

'Are you still there, Kathy? I haven't got all day. I'm beginning to wonder if the phone is playing up.'

Kathy fidgeted with her bracelet. 'Yes, I'm still here.'

'Okay, I'm all ears. If we're going to do this, let's get it done. What have you got to say for yourself this time?'

Kathy hung her head, her hair falling over her face, eyes moistening.

'I hoped you'd be glad to hear from me. I haven't rung for ages.'

'Yes, but when you do ring there's always an ulterior motive. It's never for a nice chat. You never ask how things are here with me. There's always some unspoken agenda, every single time. It's always about *you*.'

Kathy bounced a foot, her shoulders curled over her chest. 'Why so impatient, why so dismissive? If you haven't got time to talk now, I could always ring again when it's more convenient. Maybe I should make an appointment, would that suit you better? I'm sorry if I'm an inconvenience. I wouldn't want to spoil your day.'

'There's no need for sarcasm, young lady. You're on the phone now. Let's get it over with, shall we? My bath's not going to stay hot forever.'

Just say it, Kathy. Just say it and be done with it. 'I rang to tell you that I'm pregnant again.'

A deep sigh was loudly audible down the line.

'Oh, I can't say I'm surprised. Are you keeping it this time or haven't you decided?'

Kathy held the palm of her free hand to her belly, picturing the baby in her mind's eye. Wanting to protect it. Experiencing a deep love tainted with sadness.

'I want to. I *really* want to.'

'So, what does Mike think?'

Kathy felt a sinking feeling deep in the pit of her stomach.

'He doesn't know.'

Another sigh.

'Really?'

'He can't know, not this time. It has to remain a secret. That couldn't be more important. I can't stress that enough. You're the only person I've told.'

Her mother chuckled, suppressing a belly laugh fighting to be heard.

'Well, good luck with that. It tends to become rather obvious after a few months. What are you going to do then, wear a loose dress or say you've put on a bit of weight? And that was a joke, by the way, in case you were wondering. Mike's going to find out, that's the reality. There's only so long one can hide a pregnancy. Think about it, for goodness sake. You're not making any sense at all.'

'Now who's being sarcastic? I do know what happens when expecting, Mum, I'm not a complete idiot despite what everyone seems to think. I want to keep the pregnancy from him for as long as possible. That's all I'm saying. That's what I should have said in the first place.'

'Do you want me to tell you what I really think or just what you want to hear?'

'What's that supposed to mean?'

'You can't look after yourself properly, let alone a baby.'

Kathy wiped a tear from her face, smearing dark mascara across one cheek.

'I'd be a good mum if given a chance. All I need is the opportunity. I'll prove it if I can. You wait and see.'

'I wonder what goes on in that head of yours sometimes. Tell Mike now, that's my advice. He's the father. He's got the right to know, and he's going to find out soon enough anyway. Why delay the inevitable?'

Kathy's heart was pounding, thundering in her ears as if attempting to drown out her thoughts, adrenalin surging through her bloodstream.

'Have you forgotten what happened the last time I told him I was pregnant. I'd never seen him so angry. He was like a wild animal, snarling, spitting spite. The same thing would happen again. I've got no doubt in my mind. It's as inevitable as night and day.'

'That doesn't sound like the Mike I know.'

'He threw me to the floor, kicked me in the gut and I miscarried. I've explained all this. How many times do I have to repeat myself? I lost my baby because of what he did, and nobody cared but me.'

Kathy's mother rolled her eyes.

'Oh God, not this again! I thought we were done with the wild allegations. I hoped you were finally getting better. All your attention-seeking behaviour isn't going to achieve anything at all. It does nothing but damage. When are you going to realise that?'

'He's violent, Mum. He's always been violent, when we're alone, when no one's watching. He leaves bruises where no one else can see. He's hit me from the first day of our marriage. Right from the very start.'

'Then why haven't you left him? Can you answer that for me? If your allegations were more than a desperate female fantasy, you'd have gone long ago.'

'I've tried, Mum, believe me, I've tried. But he always drags me back. And then it's worse, much worse. He calls it justifiable punishment or behaviour modification therapy. That's his idea of a joke; he makes my life a living nightmare. If I could escape him, it would be the happiest day of my life.'

'Have you talked to Dr Jones recently? Maybe she could review your medication. It's got to be worth a try, hasn't it? You need help, Kathy, that's blatantly obvious to anyone. But not the kind of help you're suggesting. Talk to your doctor. You need professional help.'

Kathy was crying now. Her chest heaving as she gasped for breath.

'What m-medication? I'm not taking a-any medication. I haven't seen a doctor for ages.'

Her mother snorted. 'Well, maybe that's the real problem right there. Have you thought about that? Maybe if you did what you were told for once in your life, we wouldn't be having this conversation now. I don't know how Mike copes with it all. It's been one lie after another since the miscarriage.'

'They aren't lies. It's the truth, nothing but the truth. Why won't you believe me?'

'You need to stop this and stop it now. There's only so much anyone can put up with before they snap. I'm beginning to understand how much Mike has to deal with. It's him I feel sorry for.'

Kathy tugged at her hair.

'What on earth are you talking about?'

'Mike has told me all about your issues, Kathy. I know you've been ill since losing the baby last year. I know all about the psychiatric evaluation. And I know you're not cooperating with the treatment plan. What on earth are you thinking, girl?

It's time to start listening to the experts. That's your best chance of getting better. You do want that, don't you? Concentrate on getting yourself well and then think about a baby in a year or two when everything's on an even keel.'

Kathy tightened her grip on the phone, resisting the almost overwhelming temptation to hurl it at the wall.

'None of that's true – not a single word. It hasn't happened. I haven't seen a psychiatrist. I haven't seen anybody. Mike wouldn't allow that. It's the last thing he'd want. I might say something about what goes on here. I could show my injuries. He keeps me a prisoner in the house. I may as well spend my life in a cell. I don't go out at all.'

'Injuries? Are you talking about the self-harm you inflict on yourself to gain attention?'

Kathy shook her head, one way and then the other.

'I've got no idea what you're talking about. It's all a lie. Every single word of it.'

'Oh, come on, Kathy, you can drop the pretence. Mike's told me what you do to yourself. He's told me you've refused to join him when he visits. And he's told me you won't accept visitors at your place, not even me. It's not healthy, Kathy. You've got to start mixing again. What's cutting off your family going to achieve?'

'It's not like that. None of that's true. Mike's a liar! You shouldn't believe a word that comes out of his filthy mouth.'

She paused before responding.

'Imagine what Mike would think if he could hear the awful way you talk about him. What on earth is wrong with you? You've got a good man. A caring man who works hard and loves you despite your many flaws. That's more than most can claim. Why isn't that enough for you? Why be the drama queen? Why the constant need for attention? You've always been the same. It's time to grow up.'

Kathy's shoulders curled over her chest.

'I need help, Mum. He's violent, abusive. I don't know what more I can say to convince you.'

'Okay, so invite me over. Prove him wrong. Let's talk face to face, me, you and Mike. Let's all put our cards on the table and sort this out once and for all.'

'I can't do that.'

Her mother groaned. 'What a surprise, you won't agree to talk, so Mike was right all along just as I thought. You've got to get a grip, young lady. There's only so long he's going to put up with your constant game playing.'

'If you came, I couldn't say anything. Not in front of Mike, he'd punish me as soon as you'd left. He'd wait until we were alone to show his true colours. I could lose the baby. No, no, he'd make *certain* I lost the baby! I've never been more sure of anything in my life.'

'Do you remember all the lies you told your father and me as a teenager? We couldn't believe a word you said to us. We were loving parents. We didn't deserve that.'

'That was different. I'm not a teenager anymore.'

'Is it different, Kathy? Is it *really* different? Or are you that same manipulative girl you were back then? You're still trying to twist everyone around your little finger for the perverse pleasure it gives you.'

Kathy was murmuring her words now. Her whispered voice reverberating with raw emotion as she choked back her tears.

'One day you'll find out I'm telling the truth. One day you'll see beyond his mask. And then you'll have to believe me.'

'You do need help, Kathy, that's blatantly obvious. But not the sort of help you're implying.'

'You'll be sorry one day.'

'Is there anything else? My bath's getting cold, I'll have to top it up as it is. I don't want to waste the water.'

'Please don't tell Mike I called. I'm still your daughter. Will you do that much for me?'

'I'll think about it.'

'*Please*, Mum, I'm begging you.'

She rose to her feet.

'If I don't tell him, and it is an *if*, it's only because I think he's got enough to put up with without your antics. He's in a high-pressure job, a demanding job. He needs your support, not your criticisms and game playing. Maybe then you'd have a relationship that works for both of you.'

Kathy checked her watch, acutely aware that time was passing a lot faster than she'd like in a better world.

'So you won't tell him?'

'No, I won't tell him.'

'Do you promise?'

'If it means that much to you, yes, I promise.'

'I wish Dad was still with us.'

'Don't even go there! I'm just glad he died before seeing what you've become. He liked Mike. He was fond of him. All this would have broken his heart.'

Kathy pressed her fingers to trembling lips, tearing up again as she lowered her hand. 'Goodbye, Mum, I hope you enjoy your bath. I won't be contacting you again.'

Chapter 6

Probationary Police Constable 134 Christopher Dawson was very much hoping he wouldn't receive an answer as he knocked reticently on the Conner's front door at 8.15pm the following Tuesday evening. He wished he was almost anywhere else, doing anything else, but he had a job to do. Stress came with the territory. It's what he'd signed up for. No one had told him policing was easy. He had no choice but to do his job.

Dawson stood on the doorstep rubbing his hands together, tapping a foot against the cold and telling himself he may not receive an answer. But all too soon a white light shone brightly in the hallway, the door opened and Inspector Michael Conner stood to face him with a dour expression that said a thousand words. He looked different out of uniform – an ordinary man rather than the superman the young constable had built up in his mind. As if his identity were intrinsically linked to the blue cloth, one thing on duty when upholding the law and another thing entirely here in his private life.

'What can I do for you, constable? I hope you're not going to piss me off any more than you already have. That wouldn't be a good idea. Not unless you want to be directing traffic for the rest of your less than glittering career.'

Dawson took a deep breath, desperate to retreat but standing his ground.

'Sorry to bother you, sir. But a neighbour—'

Conner took a single step forward, placing his face only inches from the young officer's, not allowing him to finish his sentence and refusing to look away.

'Just spit it out, lad, before you get rooted to the spot. It's been a stressful evening. You're only making things worse.'

Dawson blew out a short breath which steamed in the cold night-time air.

'We've er, we've received a report of a female screaming at this address, sir.'

Conner pressed his lips together, shaking his head and sneering.

'Oh, for fuck's sake! I know where this crap has come from. It'll be that nosy git living next door, again. I've explained to him what's happening more than once. I've spelt it out in simple language that even that moron should be able to understand. I think he must be getting senile or something. I'd like to shut him up once and for all. The man's a fucking menace.'

'Can I come in and talk, sir?'

'No, you fucking well can't. Everything is just fine and dandy, no problems here. I suggest you piss off and leave me in peace. There's a good lad. Best be on your way.'

Dawson felt his face reddening as his pulse began to quicken, dark sweat patches forming under both arms despite the chill.

'I can't do that, sir. You know that. I've got a job to do.'

Conner laughed, head back, Adam's apple protruding in his throat.

'Well, aren't you the little do-gooder, PC Plod? Stay there, don't move an inch, and I'll go and get the missus. You can speak to her in person if that makes you happy. She's as mad as a fucking hatter, but you might get some sense out of her if you're lucky. Perhaps then you'll be satisfied and get some idea of the shit I'm dealing with on a daily basis.'

'Thank you, sir. You know it makes sense.'

Conner glared at him, turning away without a response, striding down the hallway before disappearing into the sitting room to his left, slamming the door behind him.

Kathy stood cowering, half-hidden behind a floral armchair, making herself smaller. 'I d-didn't ring the police. Honestly, I didn't r-ring. It wasn't me. I wouldn't make that mistake again. Not after the last time.'

Conner placed his face next to hers, foreheads touching, hissing his words, spraying her with tiny globules of warm saliva that made her cringe.

'I know you didn't ring, bitch. You can stop shuddering. There's something you need to do for me.'

Kathy nodded, moving her head back a few inches before wiping her face with the sleeve of her cardigan.

'What is it? Just tell me what to do, and I'll do it. Anything you say.'

He sighed.

'Right, you're going to pull yourself together and then you're going to tell that moron standing at the door that you're absolutely fine. In fact, you've never felt better in your entire life. We had a minor disagreement, and you got worked up about nothing at all. Whoever called the police was mistaken. There is nothing whatsoever to worry about. Do you think you can manage that much for me? Do you think that's within your gift?'

'Yes, I think so.'

He shook his head, slowly, deliberately.

'Oh, you *know* so, bitch, you *know* so, thinking's not enough.'

Kathy lowered her gaze.

'Yes, yes, that's right, I know so. I definitely know so. Just like you said. Anything you say.'

Conner clutched her tightly by a forearm, digging in his thumbs, pulling her upright so that she was balancing on tiptoes.

'Right, time to get it done. I want him gone and quickly. Do not fuck this up, Kathy. It won't go well for you if you do.'

She focussed on the floor.

'I'll do my best.'

He increased his grip a little tighter.

'Oh, I know that, Kathy. Because you know the consequences of screwing up again. Now get out there and put on an award-winning performance. I'll be watching and listening to every single word that comes out of your stupid mouth. If there's even the slightest suggestion that there's a problem, you'll pay a heavy price. It would mean the worst punishment you've ever experienced.'

Kathy fastened the top two buttons of her cardigan, opened the lounge door with quivering fingers and made her slow, weary way down the hall towards the front door. A part of her wanted to call for help. A part of her wanted to scream for help and tell the young officer the grim reality of her situation in graphic detail he couldn't choose to ignore however much he wanted to. But experience held her back. She'd made that error before. That's what she told herself. Her manipulative bastard husband would find some way of explaining whatever she said away, as if nothing at all of significance had happened. He'd worm his way out of it just as he always did. He'd get away with his crimes and blame her in the process. He was good at it, skilled. Such things defined him. There was no escaping the fact. She had to do precisely what he'd ordered. Nothing less was acceptable.

'Hello, officer. Sorry to leave you standing in the cold. How can I help you?'

Dawson forced a quickly vanishing smile, asking himself why she'd taken so very long to enter the hall.

'I just wanted to make sure you're okay, Mrs Conner. A neighbour thought he heard you screaming earlier in the evening. He seemed genuinely concerned that you may have been injured in some way.'

Kathy adopted a puzzled expression, folding her arms across her chest.

'Oh, really, he needn't have concerned himself. There's absolutely nothing to worry about, nothing at all.'

'Were you screaming?'

What could she say to that? That's what she asked herself as she stood and stared with a blank expression on her face.

The constable's eyes narrowed.

'Are you okay, Mrs Conner? Is there anything I can do to help you? All you have to do is ask. I'm here to assist you if I can.'

Kathy tugged at her hair before lowering her hand, holding his gaze right up to the time it was no longer comfortable. 'I'm absolutely fine, thanks. Nice of you to ask. I get worked up sometimes, over not very much at all. I don't know what's wrong with me. It's not a matter for the police; my husband's looking after me. What more could I want than that? He really is a wonderful partner.'

Dawson took a contact card from the top pocket of his navy tunic, held it out, but then withdrew his hand quickly when she didn't accept it.

'You can ring me at any time at the station if you need to. I'm sure you know the number as well as I do. If you need any assistance of any kind, please don't hesitate to call.'

Kathy felt her facial muscles tighten, changing the contours of her face. Why isn't he going away? I've said what I needed to say. Why on earth isn't he going?

'That won't be necessary, but thank you anyway. It's nice of you to think of me. But I'm sure you've got much more important things to be getting on with. I've got my very own police officer here in the house. Why would I need you or anybody else?'

Dawson was about to speak again, still not entirely persuaded, when Inspector Conner suddenly re-entered the hallway, walking towards them, loose-limbed, attempting to portray as relaxed a persona as possible.

'Are you happy now, constable? Are you going to piss off and leave us in peace? Surely, there must be some criminals that need catching once you've had enough of wasting your time here. What do you say, Kathy? Should PC Dawson fuck off and let us get back to the telly?'

'Yes, yes, he should. I've wasted enough of his time already.'

'Did you hear the lady, constable? I think she made herself crystal clear, don't you?'

Dawson nodded. 'Yes, I heard her, sir.'

'Then that should tell you all you need to know.'

'I'll be on my way, sir. Thank you for your time, Mrs Conner. You know where I am if you need me.'

'She's not going to need you, son, she's told you that. Now piss off and do something useful for once in your life.'

'Goodnight, sir, I'm sorry to have bothered you.'

Michael Conner's contempt was palpable as he slammed the door shut and shoved Kathy back in the direction of the lounge.

'Did you like him, bitch? Did you like your knight in shining armour? Or did you decide that he's as fucking useless as you are?'

Chapter 7

Detective Sergeant Sarah Hodgson was tucking into a much-anticipated prawn and mayo sandwich when Christopher Dawson spotted her across the busy police canteen. He waved exuberantly, approaching her table with a mug of steaming tea in one hand and a plate of double egg and chips in the other. 'Can I have a quick word please, sarge? There's something that's bothering me.'

Hodgson swallowed a mouthful, washing it down with a slurp of tap water, smiling without parting her lips. 'Yeah, no probs. Pull up a chair and take the weight off.'

Dawson shifted uneasily in his seat. 'I've got to be honest, sarge… I was in two minds about saying anything at all.'

'If something's bothering you, you need to tell me. I'll help if I can. How does that sound?'

He frowned, linking his fingers in front of him as if in prayer.

'I was called to Inspector Conner's home a couple of nights back.'

'And?'

'A neighbour rang in to say he'd heard a woman screaming. There was one hell of a racket apparently. It had all calmed down by the time I got there. I don't feel I got to the bottom of it.'

'I read the paperwork. You spoke to Mrs Conner, she said she was okay, and that was the end of it, yeah… job done.'

Dawson's eyes narrowed.

'I think there may be more to it, sarge. It's been playing on my mind ever since. I can't shake off my misgivings. I only wish I could.'

'Okay, tell me more.'

'I checked the records. It was the fifth time we've been called to the house in a little over eighteen months. Twice by Mrs Conner herself and three times by the same concerned neighbour. It was the second time in less than a fortnight. If we were dealing with anyone else we'd have done something long before now, wouldn't we? We'd have taken a formal statement, maybe made an arrest. I've completed the domestic violence training. It seems obvious. The woman needs help.'

Hodgson tapped the table three times.

'Now look, I know where you're coming from, but you need to be very careful what you're insinuating. I checked the records myself a while back. I was as concerned as you are until I knew the full story. Assumptions can be dangerous in police work. Situations can be far more complex than they first appear. You need to understand that this is one of those cases.'

Dawson unlinked his hands then sat back in his chair, still far from persuaded.

'So, what's it all about?'

'Mrs Conner is suffering from serious mental health issues. Paranoia, depression, flashbacks, anger issues – even hearing voices. Inspector Conner has told me all about it. It's terrible really. I knew her before she got ill. She was a lovely girl in those days, full of life, bright, intelligent, with a great sense of humour. She wanted to be a primary school teacher. She'd even applied for the course. Then it all went horribly wrong.'

'So, what happened to her?'

Hodgson's expression darkened.

'It all started when she lost the baby. They were both desperate to become parents, but she had an unexplained miscarriage. It sometimes happens when it's least expected. It hit them both hard, but in Mrs Conner's case the grief triggered a complete mental meltdown.'

He frowned hard.

'Can grief do that?'

'I'm no expert but, yeah… it seems so. Her decline was sudden and dramatic, from what I'm told. The baby's loss blew their lives apart. Mike seems to have come to terms with what happened to some degree, but Kathy can't move on. She hasn't been the same since. That one event seems to have ruined their lives.'

Dawson swallowed a gulp of tea, his mind travelling back in time. He was there again, at the Conner's house, looking Kathy Conner in the eye.

'I hear what you're saying, but I spoke to the woman face to face. She seemed sane enough to me.'

'How long for? Think about it for a moment. How long were you actually talking to her?'

'Well, a minute perhaps… two minutes maximum. We were standing at the open door. I didn't have a chance to enter the house and speak to her at any length.'

Hodgson placed her elbows on the table, leaning towards him, holding his gaze.

'Yeah, exactly, just a minute or two! Think about what you're saying. You're no more expert than me, Chris. You're a working copper, not a social worker or psychologist. Do you really want to rock the boat on the basis of a fleeting first impression?'

'The woman seemed frightened enough to me. I got the distinct impression that she was shitting herself the entire time she was talking to me. And the inspector was seriously pissed off. He made that perfectly clear. He didn't want me there one little bit. He was quite intimidating, to be honest. I hadn't seen that side of him before.'

Hodgson jerked her head back.

'Look, Chris, I don't know what part of this you're not getting. You've got to understand that Mike's had a great deal to put up with, the poor sod. I don't know how he manages to stay as cheerful as he does. I don't think I could handle the situation nearly as well as he does. I'd have walked away long ago. Most people would have. But he's stood by her. He offers his wife what support he can despite all the hassle she gives him. He deserves a frigging medal. The last thing he needs is us poking our noses in and making things even worse than they already are.'

'I don't know, sarge. It just didn't feel right. Cheerful's the last word that springs to mind, not on that night anyway. There was a definite tension in the air.'

Hodgson pushed her empty mug aside, wiping her mouth with the back of one hand.

'I don't know what else I can say to you, Chris. I've explained the situation, but you don't seem to be listening to what I'm telling you. You're pretty new to the job. You haven't got much experience dealing with this sort of thing. Take what I've said on board and leave it at that, that's my advice.'

'It's a gut feeling and it's nagging away at me.'

She glared at him, making her displeasure obvious.

'Well, so much for a relaxing lunch. Thanks a bunch. We could pay Mrs Conner a joint visit to satisfy your concerns if you really think it would help. But it's not going to do either of us any favours when you're proved wrong. You need to realise that. People like Mike – they respect him. You're not going to be the flavour of the month if you wade in again and give him even more problems than he's already got. I can tell you that much. You'd be a pariah. The least popular officer in the division. But if you insist, if you won't let the matter lie, I'll be at your side, God help me.'

He blew the air from his mouth, his mind racing.

'Come on, Chris, it's decision time. Are we going to pay her another visit? What do you want to do? It really is up to you.'

Dawson shifted his gaze to the wall.

'No, I don't think so, sarge, I'm sure you're right. I was sounding off, that's all. You know, thinking out loud. If you're certain there's nothing criminal going on, I'll happily leave it with you. You're a better judge than me.'

Hodgson pressed a palm to her heart. 'You've made the right decision. The inspector's got enough shit to deal with without us stamping all over his private life. And it wouldn't do Mrs Conner any favours either. She's got enough stress in her life. She sees a psychiatrist for therapy on a regular basis. Mike told me that himself. Best leave helping her to the experts. That's what they're there for. There's only so much we can do.'

'You won't tell the inspector what I said, will you?'

Hodgson looked the young probationer in the eye and smiled, making him wait. 'Go and get me another coffee and I'll think about it.'

'Thanks, sarge, you're a star.'

'Oh, and buy me a jam doughnut if you want to seal the deal. This job can be gut-wrenching at times. I could do with a bit of cheering up.'

Chapter 8

'**W**oof, woof, Battersea Dogs Home.'

Kathy smiled as happy memories of times long gone flooded back. 'Hilarious as always, sis, how are you doing?'

'Where've you been? You haven't rung for ages.'

'Well, I'm ringing now.'

'I've tried phoning you loads of times, but all I get is a "number not in service" message. I thought it might be some temporary fault, but I gave up in the end.'

Kathy nodded in reflexive response.

'Yeah, Mike has changed the number again, ex-directory as usual. I don't even know it myself. I couldn't give it to anyone however much I wanted to, and that suits him just fine. It's the third time he's done it this year.'

'And you still haven't got a mobile?'

'You have got to be kidding me. He'd never let that happen. Not in a million years.'

'I've thought of visiting unannounced when he's likely to be in work, but, well… you know what I'm saying. I didn't want to risk it. Not after the last time.'

Kathy frowned. 'Yeah, I think that's sensible. He doesn't always park on the drive. I think it's a way of catching people out. He sets traps and then punishes me for the slightest reason.'

'It doesn't get any better, does it?'

'No, it certainly doesn't. Mike's not an easy man to live with.'

Anna laughed despite the tension. 'That has got to be the understatement of the bleeding century. He's an absolute bastard! Difficult doesn't even begin to describe him.'

'Yeah, you won't hear me arguing.'

'So, where's Mike now?'

'At work, as far as I'm aware.'

'So, it's safe to talk?'

'Yeah, the phone bill only arrived a couple of days back. I've got almost three months before he checks the next one. That gives me more than enough time.'

'More than enough time for what, exactly?'

Kathy counted slowly to three inside her head, pondering her choice of words, unsure of how much to share.

'I need your help, Anna. This isn't a social call. I risked phoning you for a reason.'

'Whatever you need. You only have to ask. You should know that. I've said it before. I'm willing to do anything I can to help.'

'I'm pregnant again.'

Kathy could hear a sharp intake of breath from the other end of the line before her sister responded.

'Are you certain?'

Kathy shuffled her feet.

'Yeah, I've done a test. The bastard raped me. There's no room for doubt.'

'Oh God, that's awful! Does he know?'

Kathy shook her head, eyes darting towards the window as a car horn sounded in the road outside. She stilled herself and listened, relaxing slightly as it drove on.

'No, and we've got to keep it that way. I want to keep this one safe. And I'm going to do whatever it takes to that end. If I lose another child, it won't be without a fight.'

'Okay, so what do you need from me?'

'You do realise that he'll come after you if he finds out you've helped me, don't you? He won't let it go. He never lets anything go. He hasn't got a forgiving bone in his body.'

'Yes, I hate to admit that he had me conned for a time, but I know you better than anyone. I know when you're telling the truth. I've tried telling Mum what you're going through. I've tried convincing her what Mike's really like, but she doesn't want to hear it. She swallows every word that comes out of his lying mouth. It's like he's got her brainwashed or something. She seems to think the sun shines out of the bastard's arse.'

Kathy closed her eyes tight shut.

'Yeah, I've tried reaching out to her, but I never get anywhere. Mike's a good manipulator, that's the truth of it. He's played Mum perfectly. But I'm not all alone with my problems, and I'm grateful. Just knowing you're there makes me feel better. If it weren't for you, I'd have given up long ago. I'm grateful I've got you, sis.'

'Don't be so daft. Of *course*, I'm here for you. Best friends forever. Just like when we were kids, you and me against the world.'

'I wish Dad was still with us. Things would have been different. He'd have done something to intervene, made things right. And Mum would have listened to him whatever Mike said.'

Anna fingered her necklace, repeatedly revolving a glass bead between her fingers.

'Yes, I miss him terribly.'

'If only every man was like him. He had our backs. He always put us first.'

Kathy hesitated as the past faded.

'Mike is changing, Anna – and not for the better. The violence is getting worse almost by the day; it's escalating. And he seems to enjoy it more than before. He's becoming more sadistic, increasingly cruel. The more pain I'm in, the greater my fear and distress, the more he seems to like it. It excites him as nothing else can. It's what turns him on. It's the *only* thing that turns him on. He can't get hard without inflicting suffering. If I don't escape soon he'll end up killing the baby and maybe me too. It really is that bad.'

'Jesus… has it really gotten that awful?'

Kathy massaged her bruised ribs, deep in reflective thought.

'I've got to get out of here for good this time. To somewhere Mike can't ever find us. It's our only chance. If he finds out I'm pregnant and can get his hands on me… well, you know what I'm saying. I've explained what he did the last time. The child never stood a chance, and this one won't either. He'd make certain of that. He'd do whatever it takes and not worry about the consequences.'

'He seems capable of getting away with almost anything.'

'Yeah, yeah, he does. He's got almost everyone conned. No one else seems able to see past the mask. We're the only two people who know the reality.'

'What are you going to do?'

'This is going to seem like a strange question, but are you still working for the Blood Transfusion Service?'

Anna rubbed the back of her neck.

'Well, yes, I am, but what the—'

'That's what I hoped you'd say. I want you to take my blood, as much as possible and as soon as possible.'

Anna touched her parted lips.

'Are you saying you want to donate? It's laudable, particularly given everything you're going through, but how's that going to help you? Perhaps now isn't the best time. You've got more than enough to worry about without adding to your burdens. And it's best not to donate when you're pregnant. Let's talk about it again when you're safe. How does that sound?'

'No, it's *absolutely* essential, Anna! It's… it's something I *have* to do. It really couldn't be more critical. I can't stress that enough.'

Anna jerked her head back.

'Okay, if you say so. But Mike's not going to like it. The last thing he'd want is the two of us getting together. Surely it's going to make your situation worse, not better.'

'This is something I need you to do for me, whatever your misgivings. I want you to come here to the house and do exactly what I've asked of you.'

'You're not going to change your mind about this, are you?'

'No, no I'm not.'

'Okay, when?'

Kathy's posture slumped, a slow smile replacing a scowl.

'Mike's away on a course for two days from this coming Monday. I only know because he left the letter on the sideboard this morning. It's my lucky break, my winning ticket. I've got to make the most of the opportunity while I can. This is it, Anna. I might not get another chance. We need to take full advantage.'

'I get that you want to leave, who wouldn't? But what's the blood donation all about? You're not making a lot of sense. And why risk it when you've got a baby on the way? Are you certain you've thought this through properly?'

'Do you trust me?'

'Of course, I do. It goes without saying. I always have and I always will.'

'Then please accept it when I tell you it's best not to know what I'm planning. No more questions, okay? Just do what I ask and leave it at that. It's better that way. I'll take care of the rest. You'll understand when it's done.'

'This has got to be the strangest conversation we've ever had, but I'll do what I can. You deserve to be happy.'

Kathy stared into the distance.

'This is it. It's really happening. And there's no going back this time. Not once we've started. Are you sure you want to be a part of it?'

'I've got no idea what you're up to, but yes, I want to help. When do you need me there?'

Kathy punched the air in silent triumph.

'Monday morning after he's left the area. Let's say ten o'clock if that's all right with you?'

'I'll have to book some time off work. But, yeah, I'll be with you at ten sharp.'

'Please don't come a second earlier. If he spots your car anywhere near the house, he'll come back to check it out. And that would be the end of it. My plans would be in tatters before they'd even started.'

'I'll bear it in mind.'

'Have you got everything you're going to need? All the equipment?'

'Yes, no problem, that's not an issue, I keep it all in the boot of the car.'

'How much blood can you take?'

'It's usually 460 ml per donation.'

'What's that in old money?'

'It's a bit less than a pint.'

'How do you store it?'

Anna laughed despite, or perhaps due to, the emotive nature of the conversation.

'This is a bit like being on *Mastermind*. Specialist subject, the Blood Transfusion Service.'

'So what's the answer, for one point?'

'It's kept in specially produced bags.'

'And it doesn't coagulate?'

'The bags contain an anticoagulant. It's not an issue unless the blood's subjected to the air. And that's not going to happen unless one splits open.'

'Okay, so, how's it stored?'

'It's just kept chilled. Nothing complicated. Why on earth are you asking?'

'So, I could keep it outside at this time of year, yes? That wouldn't be a problem?'

'It wouldn't be ideal, but yes… I guess so during the colder months, if you really wanted to. But why would you? Aren't I going to be taking it away with me? That's the usual routine. I take the blood, drop it off at the collection point, that's the norm.'

'Not this time.'

'You're planning on keeping it there?'

'Yes, somewhere Mike can't find it. It's the only way my plan is going to work.'

Anna fumbled with the phone.

'Okay, if you say so.'

'Thank you!'

'Anything that helps.'

Kathy cried out in release. Things were going her way at last.

'I'm going to need a pair of those thin rubber gloves. I don't know what they're called.'

'Do you mean surgical gloves?'

'Yeah, that's the ones I'm talking about. Can you get them for me?'

'Well, yes, of course I can. But what on earth is this all about, Kathy? If you weren't my sister, I'd be putting the phone down at this point.'

'I can't tell you. Please accept that. But I know what I'm doing. I've thought it through very carefully. I've got a detailed plan and I think it can work. It will all make perfect sense to you once I'm done.'

'This is all getting too weird for words.'

Kathy held her breath. 'But you'll do it, yes? You'll bring everything with you as we've discussed?'

'I guess so if it matters that much to you.'

'I can't get away without your help. It's as simple as that.'

'Okay, I've said I'd bring everything and I will. No questions asked.'

Kathy stumbled back on wobbly legs, slumping into the nearest chair. 'Thanks, sis, I'm truly grateful. Park well away from the house. That's important! The old bloke living next door's a right curtain twitcher. He tries to help. He's phoned the police on my behalf more than once. But he's best kept out of it given the dangers. He may even talk to Mike and give you away without ever realising the damage he'd caused. And don't knock. He may hear you and stick his nose in. I'll leave the back door open. Just come in quietly, and I'll be ready and waiting. Understood?'

'Absolutely, every single word.'

'That's good to hear.'

Anna raised a hand, brushing her fringe away from her eyes, laughing nervously. 'I'll see you on Monday morning, Kathy, even if it is the strangest request you've ever made. Is there anything else you're going to need? Now's the time to tell me if there is. It'll be too late once I'm there.'

Kathy paused, her voice hesitant when she finally broke the silence. 'There is one thing.'

'Okay, what is it?'

'I'm completely skint. Mike doesn't allow me access to money, not a penny. I can order food online with his express permission, but that's it. It's his account, his card. If I used it for anything else he'd be quick to find out. I'd never get away with it. He'd beat me to a pulp. I hate to ask, but is there any chance of a small loan? I can't think of any other way of getting what I need to get away.'

'How much are we talking?'

'Um, maybe two or three hundred pounds. Would that be possible? I can't say when, but I'd pay you back as soon as I could. You know I'm good for it.'

'How does five hundred quid sound? I've got that much in my Post Office account. It's the best I can do without talking to Tom.'

Kathy beamed. 'Thanks, sis, that would be wonderful. I really appreciate your help. I won't forget this. You're a lifesaver.'

Anna took a deep breath, sucking the air deep into her lungs. 'You're my sister and need my help. What else would I do?'

'It's my only way out.'

'Oh, and one last thing. Make sure you've eaten something and have plenty to drink before I get to the house, non-alcoholic. If we're going to do this, we're going to do it properly.'

'So it's happening.'

'Yes, it seems so.'

Kathy punched the air for a second time, dancing in a tight circle.

'Sometimes, exceptional circumstances demand extraordinary actions. This is one of those times. Do or die, life or the grave. I just hope I can escape Mike's clutches, for my sake and the baby's too. If I can get everything right, there are better times ahead.'

'I'll keep my fingers crossed.'

'And everything else!'

'I'll see you on Monday, sis. Stay strong, and you'll win in the end.'

Chapter 9

Kathy's mind drifted into a morbid daydream almost as soon as she put down the phone and wiped away her fingerprints. Mike was watching her every move with prying eyes; listening to her every word with ears that heard everything. He knew all about her plan of escape and all about the pregnancy too. He knew everything he needed to know to stop her in her tracks, condemning her to a life of unbridled misery even worse than before.

Kathy screwed up her face, picturing her husband striding towards her, a glint in his eye, the white tester clutched tightly in one hand, knowing, hateful, radiating destructive intention from every pore as he got nearer. He was forming his hands into tight fists, weapons. Raising one in the air, foaming at the mouth like a rabid beast. And then he hurled the tester to the floor, drew his arm back and punched her hard, bang – right on the point of her chin, splitting her lip with his knuckles. He lurched forwards, grabbing her tightly by the throat as she stumbled backwards, hurling her to the floor and stamping down on her abdomen time and again, murderous, cruel, worse than ever before.

Kathy was weeping now as she pictured the scene, the indisputable horror of it all, too graphic as moving pictures played behind her eyes like a cinematic film she was desperate not to watch. Mike was laughing at her, belly laughing. And laughing at her dead child too, as if it were the greatest joke of his life; the funniest thing he's ever encountered. How could he? What the hell was wrong with the man, if *man* was an appropriate description for him. The bastard, the absolute bastard! There was no choice but to escape him. She had to run and keep running, never looking back.

Kathy looked up at the clock, suddenly back in the present, cold but sweating, crying and quivering as the likely ramifications of failure fully sank in. Was it a vision of the future? That's what she asked herself. It could be, if he caught her, if he discovered her intentions. If she made even the slightest mistake. What to do? What on earth to do? Backing down wasn't an option. There was no room for the status quo – no place for retreat. Her life had changed forever, for good or bad. It was just a matter of how.

Kathy seriously considered picking up the phone and dialling her sister's number for the second time, but she quickly decided that she'd asked enough of her. If she were to obtain the last piece of the jigsaw, she was going to have to do it herself. The burden was hers and hers alone. It was *her* plan, hers to implement, whatever the consequences. She had to get her head down, do exactly what she'd thought through and face the inevitable shitstorm coming her way. Maybe, just maybe, she'd come out on top.

Kathy stood in the open doorway, glancing to the left and right, repeatedly checking the street with quick, darting eyes before finally exiting the house and closing the front door behind her for the first time unsupervised in a little over five years. She was doing the right thing, wasn't she? Surely she was doing the right thing. What other choice was there? She had to get it done, one determined step at a time. Life or death, do or die. Just as she'd thought before. Just as was imprinted on her mind, never to be erased. A statement or slogan she'd never forget. It really was as simple as that.

As Kathy hurried down the street, her coat collar raised, woollen hat pulled low to mask as much of her face as possible, she knew it was the biggest gamble of her life. A last throw of the dice. She flinched at the sight and sound of every passing car and every pedestrian going about their day. Every driver and passer-by became her husband in her mind's eye. Every face distorted and morphed into his. Every sound became an all too familiar threat screaming in her ears to pound her down a little further and undermine her confidence. I'm going to kill you, bitch. And I'm going to kill the brat, too, with a stamp or a punch you can't hope to avoid. You're not fooling anyone. I'm coming after you, faster and faster. Run, Kathy, run. You're not going anywhere. Too slow, bitch. Far too slow. You're never going to get away, not now, not ever. You can never escape me. We're destined to be together until your dying day.

Kathy increased her pace, flinching, attempting to focus on her ultimate goal as her anxiety threatened to overwhelm her at the worst possible time. Come on, Kathy, keep going, girl. Don't listen. It's not real. It's only your overactive imagination playing tricks again – the monster man's looming shadow dragging you down. Just keep walking, one step, then another, then another and repeat. That's it! You can do it. Stick to the side streets. Keep your head down. Look at the pavement. He's at work and miles away. It's not him. It's not him. He's somewhere else entirely. Don't let the bastard win.

It took Kathy a little over ten minutes to walk the approximate one-mile journey to her local health centre on the outskirts of the city she thought of as home. When the modernist 1970s red-brick building finally came into view, she quickly approached the entrance, experiencing feelings of immense relief that left her giddy. Oh, thanks be to God, she'd made it! Just as she'd hoped. Just as she'd pictured in her mind as she'd lay awake at night, planning and scheming, scared to believe her dreams could ever become a reality. And now here was the surgery in front of her. Beckoning, undeniable, ready to welcome her in. It was almost impossible to contemplate.

Kathy pushed open the heavy door and stumbled into the reception with the comparative relief of a marathon runner crossing the finishing line. But her feelings of triumph were short-lived as she glanced around, turning her entire body in small, furtive movements, as opposed to her head. The room was full of waiting patients with their aches, pains and snuffles. One, two, three… oh no, there were eleven people in total, just sitting there watching, or feigning disinterest. She hadn't considered that possibility. All those prying eyes, staring at her, snooping. There was nowhere to hide. They could see her as clear as day. Maybe he had spies everywhere. People who'd report back. People who'd sell her out without any thought for her safety or the life of her child. He'd said as much. He boasted about his informers, his collection of snitches. Maybe it was true.

Kathy slowly approached the glass reception screen, allowing the wooden counter to support her weight as her head began to swim. Come on, Kathy, hold it together, girl. You've got this far. Don't give up now. Not now, not when you're so near to achieving your goal.

She had to stay positive. Hope for the best. Maybe this time the cruel intentions of fate would pass her by.

'Can I help you, madam?'

Say it, Kathy. Just say it. They've all seen you now.

'I'd like to see Dr Jones, please.'

'Are you one of Doctor Jones's patients?'

Kathy nodded frantically.

'Yes, yes I am, it's u-urgent. Please, I'm not feeling at all well.'

The receptionist stiffened.

'Name?'

Kathy lowered her head, whispering her name, fearing someone may overhear and give her away.

'I didn't quite hear you.'

Kathy repeated herself, craning her head forward, slightly louder this time.

'Okay, thank you. Why do you need to see the doctor?'

'Why are you asking so many questions? Why the inquisition? Are you one of his spies? Is that it?'

The receptionist's mouth fell open as Kathy fought and failed to retain her composure.

'I only asked why you need to see the doctor. It's a simple enough question. There was nothing else implied. It's something I ask everyone.'

Kathy clung to the counter's edge with frantic fingers, eyes blurring as her blood pressure spiralled, the stars returning to circulate her head. She increased her grip, but her efforts were never going to be enough to prevent her from falling as her legs buckled under her. She hit the floor hard, knees first, followed by her head. She lay there, oblivious to the sudden surge of activity as the receptionist shouted for assistance. A navy-clad practice nurse arrived first, followed a minute later by a doctor, who looked on as the sister checked Kathy's breathing and pulse, placing her in the recovery position. Both professionals relaxed as Kathy's colour slowly returned to normal. The minor crisis would soon be over. Resuscitation wasn't required.

Kathy awoke lying on an examination table in a small, cluttered cream-painted room she hadn't seen before. The doctor was standing over her and listening to her heartbeat through a stethoscope, the shiny steel end of which felt cold on Kathy's skin.

'Ah, it's good to have you back with us, Mrs Conner. There's nothing to worry about, nothing whatsoever. You had a panic attack and fainted, that's all. Now, take your time and sit up for me? I've completed my examination; you're quite safe. Come on, up you get.'

Kathy rolled over onto one side, searching for a non-existent clock. 'What's the time?'

Dr Jones glanced at her watch.

'It's ten past two.'

'Oh, thank God. I've still got time.'

'That's it, Mrs Conner, try to relax. You sit there for a minute or two and get your bearings. I think that's best. Now tell me, what's the reason for your visit? I haven't seen you for what... two years?'

'I think you'll find it's almost three.'

The GP glanced at her computer screen.

'Really, as long as that?'

Kathy nodded.

'I believe so. My husband brought me for a smear test. He did most of the talking.'

'So, what can I do for you today? The receptionist mentioned that you seemed somewhat distressed when you first arrived. Now would be a good time to tell me all about it.'

'I can't sleep.'

'How long have you been having the problem?'

'It feels like ages.'

'Days, weeks, months?'

'Months, definitely months!'

'Okay, then it's high time we did something about it. There are a few practical measures I can recommend that should help. It's just a matter of trial and error until we find what works best for you.'

Kathy averted her eyes to the wall.

'My husband beats me. He's violent. I need some sleeping tablets. If I don't get some sleep soon, I'll lose my mind.'

Jones paused before responding, mulling over the revelation, weighing it up, attempting to decide if the allegations were credible.

'I'm very sorry to hear that. How long has it been going on?'

'He punched me in the ribs after the party on our wedding day. I'd smiled at a waiter, apparently. That's all it took. Everything changed from that moment. Mike became a different person overnight. I thought it was a one-off at first, an aberration, an inexplicable departure from the norm. But then it happened again the very next day. He punched me in the gut because a shirt he wanted to wear wasn't washed and ironed to his satisfaction. I was walking on eggshells after that, always cautious about what I said or did. I soon came to realise that his prior persona had been a deception, a manipulation created to con me and everyone else around him. It's something he's good at. Only I see the monster behind the mask.'

The doctor winced, oblivious to her expression as she made some notes in scribbled, barely decipherable black script.

'I had no idea.'

'Why would you? Not even my mother believes me. He hides it well.'

'Have you talked to the police about all this?'

Kathy snorted.

'He is the police.'

Jones stopped writing, bouncing the tip of the pen on her knee before speaking again.

'Ah, yes, Inspector Michael Conner, I've met him both professionally and socially. He's always seemed like such a nice person. Not at all the type of man I'd suspect of being violent towards a partner.'

'That's exactly my point, he's a Machiavellian, cunning, scheming, dripping with insincere charm. He's lied to everyone, you included. It's what he does.'

'I understand what you're telling me. I get it. You're claiming he's not what he seems.'

Kathy held her hands out wide. '*Claiming*, what's that supposed to mean? Please don't say you don't believe me either. That would be too much to bear.'

'I'm sorry, that was the wrong choice of words.'

'I've told you nothing but the truth. Every single word.'

A flush crept across the doctor's cheeks.

'I can refer you to a counsellor if you think that may help. And there are various women's charities who provide excellent services. I could write a letter if you agree.'

Kathy tensed, her heart pounding as sweat formed on her brow despite the quarter open window.

'I really haven't got time for all this. I've got to get back to the house. I need to start cooking. If he gets even the slightest clue I've been here the consequences could be dire.'

Jones turned to the computer on her desk, staring at the screen.

'Let's make another appointment when you've got more time to talk. I think that's advisable in the circumstances.'

Kathy wanted to shout. She wanted to stamp her feet. But instead, she looked the doctor in the eye and said, 'I need to sleep.

I just want the medication. If you want me to beg I'll go down on bended knee. I need what I came here for.'

'Have you ever had thoughts of suicide, Mrs Conner?'

Kathy shook her head determinedly.

'No, absolutely not! I need to sleep, that's all. Surely that's not too much to ask?'

The GP reached out, squeezing Kathy's hand.

'I'm going to write you a prescription for two weeks' pills. But I need to see you again before I issue any further medication. They're a short-term measure, not a long-term fix. Does that sound okay to you?'

Kathy's relief was almost touchable.

'Yes, thank you, it's appreciated.'

Jones wrote the prescription and handed it over. 'You can collect the tablets in the adjoining building. Royston's Chemist has moved here from the high street since your last visit. Most patients seem to appreciate the convenience.'

Kathy smiled thinly.

'Perhaps fate is on my side for once. Didn't someone once say that fortune favoured the brave?'

'I believe they did.'

'Thank you so very much for your help. It's truly appreciated.'

'You're welcome, but no more tablets until we've spoken again, yes? As I said, they're a short-term measure and not a resolution of the problem. Think of them as a sticking plaster rather than a cure.'

Kathy slid off the examination table, supporting her weight on unsteady legs that felt ready to buckle again at any moment. She steadied herself for a few seconds until sure she could trust them.

'You won't talk to anyone about what I've said, will you?'

'Not if you don't want me to. Everything you tell me is confidential.'

'And you won't tell my husband, will you? I'd be in serious danger if you did.'

The doctor raised an eyebrow, eyes wide, the expression leaving her face as quickly as it appeared.

'No, Kathy, I won't be telling your husband, that's against the rules. I couldn't talk to him even if I wanted to. Which I don't, in case you were wondering. Everything that has been said between us is confidential. I won't be speaking to anyone else regarding your predicament without your express permission.'

Kathy stared at her, holding her gaze, refusing to look away.

'What about your staff? Will they keep their mouths shut? Will they say anything to anyone? It might get back to him if they did. That's how he operates. He has his spies.'

'It would be more than their job's worth. You needn't concern yourself in that regard.'

'You'll tell them? You'll make sure?'

'You have my word. Your records will be kept private. I take my duty of care extremely seriously. You have nothing to worry about on that score. We can talk about the best way to proceed when I next see you.'

Kathy approached the door, gripping the handle.

'Thank you, that's good to know. Time's getting on, it's rushing away from me faster than ever before. Tick-tock, tick-tock. Can you hear it, doctor? He'll be back soon after five. I need to be on my way. I'll have to start cooking.'

Chapter 10

Anna Oakes parked in a quiet tree-lined side street, retrieved her bag from the hatchback's large boot and strode purposefully in the direction of her sister's home, just as the sun broke through the mottled-grey marble clouds, painting a masterpiece of light and shade that raised her spirits.

Anna checked her watch on approaching the house, relieved to see that she'd timed it perfectly to the minute. It was at least a positive start to what threatened to be a stressful morning.

Anna walked down the fragmented tarmacadam driveway, approaching the front door, glancing towards neighbouring houses on recalling her sister's cautionary advice. She walked around the side of the semi-detached home to the back of the building, picking up her pace, keeping a keen eye out for the aforementioned neighbour, who – to her relief – didn't make an appearance.

Anna opened the back door without bothering to knock, stepping into the kitchen to be met by her sister who was in the process of preparing two cups of coffee on the worktop next to the cooker. Kathy looked up and smiled nervously.

'Hi, sis, thanks for coming. Do you still take sugar?'

Anna rested her bag on the table.

'Please, two spoonfuls. I'm a martyr to my sweet tooth. I've given up trying to cut down. I just haven't got the willpower. It's a lost cause.'

'Strange, we've always been the same, you sweet and me savoury. It's the one difference between us. Do you fancy a biscuit?'

Anna shook her head.

'No, I haven't long had breakfast, ta. But you should have one if I'm going to take your blood. I don't want you passing out on me.'

'I had some cheese and tomato on toast about twenty minutes ago.'

Anna sat herself down, accepting her cup gratefully, warming her hands.

'The bastard's gone then?'

Kathy sat on the opposite side of the pine table, an implausible smile on her face.

'Yeah, he drove off about an hour ago. I watched from the bedroom window until he finally left my sight. According to the letter the course finishes at four. It's about an hour drive, and he usually goes for a drink in the city before coming home. He shouldn't be back until five at the earliest, probably later.'

'Shame he's coming back at all.'

Kathy raised her cup to her mouth, nodding as the rising vapour warmed her face.

'Yeah, you've got that right. I wish he'd sod right off and die. I wouldn't care how just as long as he'd breathed his last. You were so lucky meeting Tom when you did. If Mike were anything like him, I'd be a very happy woman.'

'Yeah, Tom's one of the good guys.'

'The best!'

Anna tapped her bag.

'I've got everything we need.'

'The bags and the gloves?'

'Yeah, just like you said.'

'And the hair dye?'

'Yes, a nice light shade of blonde, as you asked.'

Kathy smiled again, spontaneously this time, telling herself that things were looking up, finally going her way.

'We can make a start straight after we finish our coffee, if that's all right with you?'

'What's the rush?'

'No rush, I just want to get it done.'

Anna licked her top lip.

'Oh, go on then, I'll have one of those biscuits after all.'

Kathy headed to the pantry, returning with a three-quarter-full packet of garibaldis in hand.

'There you go, help yourself. One of your favourites as I recall. They should still be in date.'

Anna took a biscuit from the packet and nibbled at a corner, savouring the sweet currants, moving the mixture around her mouth with her tongue. 'I've got absolutely no idea what you've got planned, Kathy, but I need to be sure you want to continue. I've explained that there's risks. I need to know you've thought it all through properly, that you're one hundred per cent certain you know what you're doing. It's not too late to change your mind. We can pretend none of this happened, if you like? All you have to do is say the word. I could go on my way and say nothing else about it.'

'Just eat your biscuit.'

'Are you certain, yes or no? I need to hear you say it.'

Kathy tipped her head back, draining her cup.

'Yes, Anna, I'm certain. I've never been more certain. I've decided on a plan I really think can work. There's no plan B. It's the only option left open to me. I need to get on with it before it's too late. The danger of doing nothing outweighs everything else.'

'Nice biscuits!'

Kathy smiled.

'I'm glad you like them.'

'Are you ready to make a start?'

'As ready as I'll ever be.'

Anna rose to her feet. 'Are we going to do everything here or in the lounge?'

'Give me a second. I'll just give the cups a quick swill and get them out of sight.'

'Yeah, no clues I've been here. I couldn't cope with the crap you have to deal will. Having to worry about every little detail in case the bastard catches you out. Nobody should have to live like that. It's an abomination.'

'Is there likely to be any mess when you take my blood? You know, anything Mike could spot? If he gets even the slightest clue what I'm doing, I'm screwed. It would all be over before it began.'

'No, no mess, nothing like that. I'll make certain of it. It's what I do day in, day out. If he finds anything out, it won't be because of me.'

Kathy entered the lounge first with her sister close behind.

'Where do you want me?'

'You can sit in an armchair or lie on the settee if you like. Whichever suits you best. It's up to you. Just make yourself comfortable.'

Kathy closed the curtains, switching on the light at the centre of the room before stretching out on the sofa, trying her best to relax. 'Is this okay for you?'

'Yes, that's fine. You can either roll your sleeve up or take your cardigan off, whichever's easier.'

Kathy removed her cardigan, folded it, resting it on her abdomen. 'Okay, I'm as ready as I'll ever be.'

'Right, I'm going to place a blood pressure cuff on your arm. It's needed to create a little pressure.'

Kathy held out her arm, looking away. 'Can we fill four bags today?'

Anna applied the cuff, pumping up the pressure.

'Four? No, we frigging well can't. The norm is one bag every eight weeks at the very most. And that's if you're *not* pregnant. We shouldn't really be doing this at all.'

Kathy looked very close to panic, the remaining colour draining from her already pale face.

'Oh God, that's no good to me! I need the four bags before the baby starts showing. That's an intrinsic part of the plan. And four is an *absolute* minimum. Any less and it's not going to work.'

Anna took an alcohol swab from her bag before searching for an appropriate vein and cleaning the skin.

'This is getting crazier by the minute.'

'You said you trust me. That's what you said, yes?'

Anna nodded once.

'Of *course* I do.'

'Then, let's get on with it.'

'Filling a bag every three weeks or so is going to be pushing it a bit, to say the least, but if there's no other way I guess it's just about doable. That's if you're prepared to deal with the likely negative effects.'

'What effects are you talking about?'

'I want you to start tensing and relaxing your bicep for me.'

Kathy began moving her arm up and down at the elbow.

'Like this?'

'Yes, that's it, stop for a second while I insert the needle and then start again… Yes, keep it going, up, down, up, down, that's it. You're doing beautifully.'

'You were about to tell me about the side effects?'

'Yeah, there's a risk of anaemia. You could feel weak, light-headed and have lower than usual stamina. If we go ahead with the schedule you're proposing, you're going to know about it, that's for sure. They don't recommend a minimum period for nothing.'

Kathy nodded, focussing on the doable and minimising everything else in the interests of the plan.

'Would iron supplements help? I've got some somewhere.'

'They certainly wouldn't do you any harm. But you can expect to feel like crap a lot of the time, that's a given. There's no avoiding it.'

'No change there then, my life's not exactly wine and roses.'

Anna withdrew the needle, disconnected the tube, sealed the bag carefully and handed Kathy a small, fluffy white ball of cotton wool.

'Put some pressure on that for me while I find you a plaster. That's it, with your thumb, press down hard.'

'It's crazy. He beats the shit out of me on a regular basis and yet I'm afraid of a little needle.'

Anna grinned.

'Most people are. An eighteen-stone rugby playing prop I know cries like a newborn baby every time he donates. He tried to make out it was hay fever the last time, poor sod. I told him he wasn't fooling anyone. I've never seen a man looking more embarrassed.'

'Not so tough after all.'

'Are you okay, Kathy? You're looking a little pale all of a sudden.'

'Never better.'

Anna held up the syringe and tube in plain sight. 'What do you want me to do with this lot?'

'I'll hide them once I'm back on my feet.'

'We don't usually reuse them.'

'Needs must.'

Anna walked towards the door, humming.

'I'll get a plastic bag from the kitchen, which drawer?'

'The second down, next to the sink. Mike's not going to miss one.'

'Back in a second. Sit yourself upright, and I'll make us another coffee before I head off. There's a plaster next to you on the sofa when you're ready.'

'Thanks, sis, I can't thank you enough. If there's anything I can ever do for you… well, you know what I'm saying. One day I'll return the favour.'

'We're family, Kathy. Twins. There's no charge. I only hope you know what you're doing, that's all.'

'And me too, sis, me too! It's a high-stake game I've got no option but to play. I pray my hand beats his. I'm going to do everything I can to come out on top, but there are no guarantees, not in this life. Sometimes you've got to take a risk. What other choice have I got?'

'I'll make that coffee.'

The two sisters hugged each other tightly, saying their fond farewells. As Anna handed over the cash with a 'sorry it can't be more', closed the back door and walked casually in the direction of the street, Kathy was wondering if she was doing the right thing after all. Hers was an ambitious plan. A radical plan. And there were so many things that could potentially go wrong if she made even the slightest error. If that happened… well, it didn't bear thinking about. She just had to get her head down, get on with it and hope for the best.

Kathy took her bottle of sleeping tablets from a dark corner of the saucepan cupboard, placing it in the orange supermarket carrier bag along with everything else she was going to need in the weeks to come. She stepped out into the back garden for the second time in a matter of days and looked up at the sky in silent prayer. Where on earth could she keep everything? Where best to hide them? It had to be cold. And it had to be secure. Somewhere the bastard was least likely to look. Are you going to help me, God, give me a clue? It wasn't too much to ask, was it? She needed all the help she could get.

Kathy listened intently, thinking she heard a faint but discernible voice encouraging her on. A voice emanating in the far distance, somewhere in the mysterious universe and beyond our material reality. She opened the shed's wooden door and peered in with her confidence waning as nagging doubts entered her mind. There were no obvious hiding places, nothing that sprung to mind. But there was nowhere else, nowhere suitable. Nowhere that met her requirements any better. The shed was the obvious choice. It would have to do.

Kathy winced as a bathroom light shone in a nearby building. But she relaxed slightly as the blinds closed. She was beginning to feel more confident again, boosted by her decision to act. Fortified by her proactive approach to her problems. She was doing something to save herself. And to save the baby too. That's what she said to herself. She was doing something brave, something adventurous, something worthy. There was reward in that, and the bastard didn't have a clue. That may give her the edge. It was her only advantage – a benefit she had to cling on to like a determined limpet. She had to become a roaring tigress, brave and bold. There was no room in her life for a cowering creature devoid of courage. Those days were gone.

Kathy focussed back on the task at hand, casting an eager eye over every inch of the shed's varied contents. What about inside the grass storage area of the lawnmower? It wouldn't be used again until spring. Yes, that made sense. It may work.

She lowered herself onto all fours, examining her option of choice, but she quickly decided that it didn't provide sufficient space, her disappointment clear, had anyone been there to see.

Kathy pulled herself to her feet, resisting the impulse to scream as rekindled uncertainties flooded her fragile mind. All of a sudden, things weren't going quite as well as she'd hoped. There were problems, seemingly insurmountable obstacles in her way. What if she couldn't come up with an appropriate hiding place? It would be the end of her initiative, disaster. What if there was nowhere suitable to find? What if she was as useless as he'd always said she was?

Kathy imagined her husband's mocking voice, but she drove it away. It was time to think outside the box. She'd been an intelligent girl once upon a time. A university student, an academic, before he blunted her edges. Before he crushed her self-esteem and tore her down one day at a time. All she had to do was use that same intelligence as she had in the past.

Kathy looked again, noticing that one section of the shed's uneven flooring looked loose at the back. She hurried towards it, using all her meagre strength to lift the toolbox out of the way and then utilising a red-handled screwdriver to prise a small section of wooden floorboard free. She smiled, relieved, when it came away relatively quickly, and then felt her mood and confidence surge like a geyser in full flow. That's it, Kathy, it's almost perfect. That would do just fine. And everything fitted in flawlessly with a bit of moving things around. She really couldn't have found a better hiding place however long she looked. It was a triumph over adversity. The bastard would never spot it, not in a million years.

Kathy made her final adjustments to the position of the various items, placed the board back in its original position, having to wait a minute or two to regain her strength before shifting the toolbox back on top.

Kathy looked down and stared as new doubts began to surface. Was the section of floorboard *exactly* where it had first been? Yes, not bad, spot on, in fact. And the screwdriver? What about the screwdriver? Maybe move it another inch or so to the right next to the larger of the two spanners. Yes, yes, that was better. Surely it was good enough. If the bastard spotted that, he was a miracle worker.

Kathy stood at the shed's open door, taking one final look around before hurrying back in the direction of the house. As long as no one had seen her, as long as no one reported back, she'd be fine, just fine. All she could do was continue with caution and hope for the best. No, she should *pray* for the best! Maybe this time God was listening and would act on her invocation. Perhaps this time she'd win.

Kathy checked the kitchen clock, wondering why the second hand was moving so very quickly. Just like the last time. Oh God, time was rushing on again. He'd be back soon with his judgements, criticisms and worse. It was time to prepare for his arrival. Time to start cooking. She had to keep up the pretence of normality until the time was precisely right. And then she'd do it! She'd get out of there. She'd be on her way, never to return.

Chapter 11

Kathy served her husband's full English breakfast at precisely 7.30am, cooked to culinary perfection and presented with a side order of white toast and a steaming pot of aromatic, fine ground Brazilian coffee – one of his particular favourites. There were still criticisms, there were always criticisms, but Kathy somehow managed to avoid any significant interaction right up to the time he swallowed his last mouthful, pushed his plate aside and rose to his feet with a disconcerting smirk on his very ordinary face. It was a triumph in her eyes. She'd avoided his violence. There'd been no kicks or punches and – for now – that was enough.

Michael stepped away from the kitchen table as his wife swayed from one foot to the other, wondering if the time was right to clean away the dirty dishes. He met Kathy's eyes, holding her gaze as she blinked repeatedly, but he didn't utter a word.

'Is everything okay, Mike? Is there anything else I can do for you before you leave for work?'

He turned in a tight circle, slowly and deliberately, like an inept dancer on an amateur stage.

'Am I looking suitably smart, bitch? Do you think I'll impress?'

Kathy took a backward step, pressing herself against the large larder fridge, nodding with manufactured enthusiasm, very much hoping her reply would be sufficient to satisfy his ego.

'You look every bit the successful senior professional. People can't fail to be impressed. You fit your uniform perfectly.'

He ambled towards her, first one step, then a second.

'And are *you* impressed, Kathy? Are you proud to be married to such a man?'

'Oh yes, *very* proud! I've always been very proud of you.'

Her subsequent words threatened to stick in her throat, but she says them anyway. 'I know how lucky I am. You're a wonderful husband.'

He nodded twice, seemingly satisfied.

'I'm attending a domestic violence seminar in Exeter later today. I'll be part of a working party issuing multi-agency guidance and procedures for dealing with complex cases. Oh, the irony! If the morons experienced even a tiny percentage of the shit you put me through, they'd truly understand the causes. That's the sort of course they need. They should try living with *you* for a day or two without hitting out.'

He laughed, mercury fillings in full view.

'If they could manage that, it would be a fucking miracle.'

Kathy opened her mouth, once, then twice, but couldn't find the words.

He picked up his black leather briefcase, preparing to leave.

'Nothing to say for yourself, woman? No words of wisdom to share with the various numpties I'll be forced to spend my time with, the overeducated do-gooders of this world who wouldn't know a criminal if one crept up and bit them on the arse? I feel sure they'd benefit from your almost infinite understanding of the subject. Or perhaps not? After all, you're even more stupid than they are. And that's quite an achievement in itself, believe me.'

She wanted him to go. She so desperately wanted him to go.

'What time will you be back? I'll make sure there's a meal ready.'

He searched for his car keys, finding them on the table next to his cap. 'There had better be for your sake. I should be home sometime around six. Have everything ready and waiting as per usual. And make certain it's tasty and presented well. Something that looks good on the plate. Do you think you can manage that much without another catastrophic failure?'

'Oh, it will be ready, Mike, I can promise you that much. It will be ready to serve on your arrival. All you'll have to do is eat it.'

He thought he detected an unlikely spark of defiance in her tired eyes, just for a fraction of a second before it faded away. He considered the possibility, trying to read her thoughts, but then dismissed the idea out of hand. She was broken, worn down, downtrodden and undermined. His methods had been a triumph. There was no reason to concern himself. She had, he concluded, no fight left.

Kathy slumped into the nearest armchair when her husband finally closed the door and headed for his car. She listened for the roar of the powerful engine, unwinding somewhat as she heard him manoeuvring the vehicle off the driveway and into the street. Kathy rose to her feet with a sudden burst of newfound energy, born of a combination of anticipation and hope, then hurried into the lounge where she watched from the picture window, peeping out from behind the curtains, right up to the time Conner's bright-red sports convertible disappeared from her sight.

Kathy waited for a minute or two, ensuring he wasn't about to return to catch her out as was his custom, before picking up the phone with a hand that wouldn't stop shaking. She dialled and waited, counting away the seconds until she finally heard her sister's reassuringly familiar West Country tones at the other end of the line.

'Hi, Anna, it's Kathy, is it safe to talk?'

Anna Oakes lifted a pottery mug to her mouth, sipping her sweet black coffee, savouring the honey on her tongue.

'Yeah, that's not going to be a problem. Tom's in the upstairs bathroom getting ready for work.'

'Are you certain he won't hear us?'

'Not a chance, he's got the radio on. He likes his music turned up loud.'

'I can't believe how quickly the weeks have passed. It only seems like yesterday we were sitting in my lounge and you filled that first bag.'

'Yeah, I know what you're saying.'

'This is it, the time has arrived, sis, there's no more room for delays. I'm having to wear loose clothing. There's only so long that's going to convince. And the phone bill arrived yesterday morning. He hasn't asked for it yet, but it's just a matter of time until he does. There's only so long I can keep it hidden without being caught out.'

'Are you getting out of there?'

'Yes, soon, very soon.'

Anna bounced a curled knuckle against her mouth.

'Do you need me to do anything for you?'

'No, you've done more than enough already. I'll always be grateful.'

'Well, if you change your mind, if you think of anything, anything at all, all you have to do is ask. You know where I am.'

Kathy hesitated.

'Anna, there's likely to be a great deal of conjecture in the local media in the coming days about what's happened to me. People are going to be saying and writing things that aren't true. I need you to understand that and to promise me you won't ever give the game away. By all means, tell people you knew of Mike's violence towards me, that may well help my cause. But make no mention of what we've done together. That's absolutely crucial if I'm going to escape him and stay safe. I'm *so* sorry to put that burden on you, but there's no other way. Secrecy is everything. It's central to my chances of success. And it will keep you safe too. The last thing you need is Mike finding out you've helped me. You know exactly what he's like.'

'You've got nothing to worry about, my lips are sealed.'

'You can't tell anyone, Anna, not even Tom or Mum, especially not Mum. This has to be between the two of us and nobody else, whatever people ask you. And they will, believe me, they will. The police will get involved, that's inevitable.'

'I know, I know. If anyone ever finds out what we've done together, they won't have heard it from me, guaranteed.'

'If my plan works, if I get away, I'll contact you as soon as I've settled in wherever I end up. You know, when it's safe to do so. And you mustn't try to find me. That would be dangerous for both of us. You do understand that, don't you?'

Anna wiped away a tear.

'I'm going to miss you terribly, Kathy.'

'And I'll miss you, too. But that's how it's got to be, for my sake and the sake of the baby. Can you imagine the life he or she would have if we stayed, even if the baby survived for long enough to be born? It doesn't bear thinking about.'

'Tom has just switched the radio off. He's opening the bathroom door. He'll come downstairs soon.'

Kathy choked back her tears.

'Okay, that's our key to bring our conversation to an end. I love you, Anna, and thank you. I couldn't have done this without you.'

'I love you, too. Please get back in touch as soon as you can.'

'We'll be together again one fine day. Just you wait and see. We'll have our time in the sun. And that bastard will be just a memory.'

Anna swallowed her sadness.

'Best of luck to you, sis. I hope things work out brilliantly.'

Kathy's brow furrowed and her heart ached as she forced a brittle smile.

'Yes, fingers crossed, I'm going to need all the luck I can get. There's no going back now. I've got to see it through to the end. Say a prayer for me, sis, today's the day. By tonight it should be done. If everything goes to plan, I'll be on my way.'

Chapter 12

Almost twelve weeks had passed since the initial implementation of Kathy's plan, and she was ready to take the final 460 ml of blood from her arm at two o'clock that afternoon. She'd become reasonably skilled at the necessary procedures with practice, and the insertion of the needle no longer held the fear it once had, despite it being somewhat blunter than it once was. Kathy had considered asking Anna to provide a replacement, but she decided against. The importance of minimising the risk of discovery outweighed the various potential advantages.

Kathy sat upright in a comfortable armchair, tightened the cuff, pumped her arm, inserted the needle with a minor grimace, and watched as the bag slowly filled with dark-red blood. This was it. The day she'd waited for with a heady mix of excitement and trepidation. The day she'd anticipated for three long months, as her husband's hateful behaviour deteriorated still further. The day of days had finally arrived.

Kathy stored the last bag of her blood underneath the loose wooden floorboard in the garden shed along with the others, before returning to the house with the bottle of sleeping tablets clutched tightly in one hand. She wiped her shoes on the rubber doormat, ensuring not to leave even a hint of dark earth. She checked the clock for the umpteenth time that day, and continued her preparations for her husband's eventual arrival.

Kathy decided on chicken vindaloo as her final offering, partly because it was her husband's favourite meal of all, but mainly because she thought that the pungent, aromatic flavours would best mask the taste of the ten powdered sleeping tablets she intended to include in the recipe. Kathy scratched her head as she took the various spice jars from a perfectly arranged cupboard secured to the wall to the left of the cooker. She placed the glass containers on the countertop with the labels facing outwards, looking at each in turn. Salt, turmeric powder, dried red chillies, cinnamon, garlic cloves, coriander, cumin, ginger, and green cardamons. They were all there. And she'd be adding a generous promotion of finely chopped fresh onions, coriander, and green chillis too. A delicious, heady mix of strong flavours to tantalise the taste buds. Surely not even *Mike* would spot the medication in the recipe. Surely that was beyond even his detective nous. Everything depended on her assumption being correct.

Kathy sat at the kitchen table and silently acknowledged that she was finding physical tasks increasingly demanding as she crushed one tablet after another into a fine powder with the back of a hand-me-down, tarnished teaspoon, which had once belonged to her much-loved maternal grandmother. It took Kathy almost forty minutes, much longer than she'd anticipated, to complete the task and she was panting hard, like an overheated dog in need of water, by the time she finally finished squashing the last pill to her satisfaction. She sat back, sucking in the air as she looked down at the small pile of white powder on the table in front of her. A glass of cold water, that's what she needed. And a five-minute break, that was acceptable, wasn't it? A little rest before continuing. Kathy stared at the clock yet again, focussing on the second hand, seconds becoming minutes in the blink of an eye. She had sufficient time, didn't she? Yes, yes, of *course* she did. Of course she did. A little rest was essential if she was to perform to the best of her potential. Five minutes shut-eye and then start cooking.

Kathy closed her tired eyes and began picturing the hours ahead. She rehearsed her intentions in her mind, seeing herself succeed with one necessary task after another until she finally triumphed. She repeated the mental process, meditating on her success until it felt real, as if it were actually happening in real time. She pictured it and pictured it again until she believed she really could achieve the favourable outcome she desired if she followed her plan to the letter and didn't deviate from it even for a single second. Kathy sat there for another ten minutes or so with her eyes tight shut, bouncing a foot, crossing and uncrossing her arms, unable to get comfortable, and telling herself insistently that she was doing the right thing, that she could win, that she could defeat the monster man, however great his powers, however evil his intentions. This was it, her moment, the time for rest was over. She had to start cooking.

Kathy stood at the cooker, red-faced, watching for a minute or two as the finely chopped onions slowly browned in the hot oil, before adding a generous portion of crushed garlic and the various bright, multicoloured fragrant spices that brought the concoction to life. Next, she dropped in the diced chicken, having decided to add the white powder when the cooking process was almost complete, for fear that the heat may somehow negatively affect the potency and effectiveness of the medication at the worst possible time. Kathy turned down the gas flame, dropping in the powder a little at a time. A few granules, then a few more, stirring the mixture with the same wooden spoon with which she'd made the soup only weeks before. She peered into the wok, turning off the heat as her mind drifted back in time. So much had changed since that awful day. She felt like a different person now. A more hopeful person; no longer a victim but a woman seeking control of her destiny. Or at least that was what she hoped. So much depended on her success. For her, for her child, she had to hold her nerve.

The tasty looking curry was ready and waiting, precisely as planned. That gave her more than enough time to shower, change her clothes and dye her hair blonde. She knew it was another gamble on her part. The bastard may well disapprove of her new look, with all that it entailed. But it was a risk she had to take. One more throw of the dice. She repeated the thought, encouraging herself on. And maybe the offer of curry would be enough to alleviate his anger and resentment for a time. Or perhaps not, there was no way of telling. He may well explode whatever she did or said. She just had to protect her abdomen if he hit out again. That was the best. Protect the baby. Her number one priority. And then strike back when he least expected it. It was her turn now. His turn to suffer. She had to get on.

Kathy watched through a crack in the lounge curtains as Conner drove his sports car onto the driveway at a little after 5.30pm that afternoon. Deep breaths, Kathy, deep breaths, this was it. The moment had come. Don't back down now, not at this late stage. It would all be over soon enough, one way or the other. She just had to get it done. Inaction was failure and no option at all.

Kathy rushed into the kitchen where the curry was simmering gently on the gas flame. She spooned a large portion onto a white porcelain plate with a trembling hand as she heard his key in the front door. Come on, Kathy, you can do it, girl. She moved the curry around the plate, searching for even a hint of the white powder in the mixture, as she resisted the impulse to panic. Stir it in, that's it, stir it in… perfect. It had blended in wonderfully well. The results were better than even she could have hoped. The vicious bastard wouldn't suspect a thing, would he? Nagging doubts invaded her mind. Oh God, what if he did? She felt her confidence slump. Hold it together, Kathy, hold it together, girl. Now wasn't the time to fall apart. There was too much to lose.

Mike was striding down the hall now, his heavy footsteps reverberating around the room as if to announce his arrival and beat her down a little further. She had seconds, just seconds before he appeared. Quickly, Kathy, quickly, how did it taste? Oh God, what about the taste? She took a spoon and lifted a tiny amount of the mixture to her mouth just as he opened the kitchen door. He looked her up and down, slowly, disdainfully, laughing until tears ran down his detestable, youthful face.

'What have you done to your hair, you stupid bitch? What a total numpty! You look fucking ridiculous!'

Kathy forced the flicker of a smile as he sauntered towards her, desperate to hold her nerve, urging herself on.

'I thought you'd like it, Mike. You've always said you like blonde hair. You said you fancied my sister when she dyed hers, remember?'

Conner grabbed her right ear, digging in his fingernails as he jerked her head to one side, holding it at an awkward angle, making her whimper.

'Oh I do, bitch, I do. But not when it's framing your ugly face. I like it on sexy women, women with style and grace. You're not one of those women. You're a fuck up. I don't know what the hell I saw in you in the first place. It might be an idea to shave it all off and start again.'

'But we're twins. Identical twins, we look the same.'

Mike snorted, digging in his nails a little harder.

'Your sister carries herself with confidence and style. You don't and you never will.'

Kathy glanced at him, then at his plated meal, and then at him again as he loosened his grip.

'I've made you a fresh curry, vindaloo, your favourite. Nice and hot, exactly as you like it. I thought you deserved a treat after your hard day.'

He let go of her, took off his coat and sat at the table as if nothing of any significance had happened. As if their relationship were normal. As if he was an ordinary man.

'Is there any mango chutney?'

Kathy nodded with feigned enthusiasm.

'Of course there is, sweet. I made sure of it. Take a seat, and I'll fetch it from the fridge. I'm ready to serve your meal whenever you're ready.'

'Get me a beer while you're there.'

Kathy delivered the chutney jar and a can of chilled lager to the table, followed by his plated meal, piled high.

'Are there any poppadoms?'

'Um, no... I, er, I didn't have the ingredients.'

'You are fucking useless, woman!'

'I'll make sure they're available next time.'

He lifted a forkful to his mouth.

'Oh I know you will, Kathy, because you understand the consequences of letting me down again.'

Kathy stood and watched her husband closely, full of hope as he chewed and swallowed one toothsome mouthful after another, eating with gusto.

'Is it to your taste, Mike. I can add a little more spice if you'd like it better. I'm here to serve. All you have to do is ask.'

He chose to ignore her, washing down the curry with repeated swigs of cold beer every three or four mouthfuls until his plate was almost empty.

'Would you like some more curry? You seem to be enjoying it. There's plenty more in the wok. I made more than enough for seconds.'

He yawned expansively, closing his eyes for a fleeting moment before opening them again and pushing his plate to the floor.

'Just shut the fuck up, woman. I don't know what the hell's wrong with me. I'm knackered all of a sudden. I must be going in for a bug or something. I hope it's not something I've caught from *you*.'

Kathy raised her eyebrows. This was it. The moment had come. Get the bastard upstairs before it was too late. He'd be far too heavy to carry.

'Perhaps you've been working too hard again. You're so very dedicated to that job of yours. Why don't you head to bed for an hour or two's shut-eye before the boxing's on the telly? I can bring you a nice hot-water bottle if you like? You'd like that, wouldn't you? You said the heat helps you relax.'

Conner struggled to his feet with the aid of the table, yawning at full volume.

'I don't know what the fuck's wrong with me. I'm feeling like shit all of a sudden.'

'There's a bug making the rounds. I heard a report on the local radio news.'

'I haven't heard anything.'

'Why not head up to bed? I've changed the sheets, nice and fresh. A few hours' sleep and you'll be feeling absolutely fine again. I think there's some soluble aspirins in the bathroom cabinet if you'd like some? They should do the trick.'

Conner stumbled towards the staircase on unsteady legs that felt as if he'd been anaesthetised.

'Who are you, my fucking mother?'

Kathy followed close behind him, just out of striking distance, urging him on as he lost his footing on the first step, stumbling and almost falling.

'I'm just trying to help you, Mike, that's all. Up you go. Come on, up you go. I'll fetch that hot-water bottle I mentioned as soon as you're under the covers.'

He turned his head, glaring back at her, snarling on approaching the landing, gripping the bannister with both hands for fear of falling.

'Well, don't fucking bother. You're useless, woman. And keep the noise down until I get up. Got it? I don't want to see your ugly face again unless I call you. Have you got that into your thick head?'

Kathy studied him from the comparative safety of the landing as he approached the bedroom door.

'That's it, Mike, you're nearly there. Into bed with you. Nice and snug. You'll feel much better after a bit of rest.'

He fell on top of the bed fully clothed, snoring almost immediately, oblivious to Kathy walking towards him and standing at his side.

She looked down at him.

'That's it, you bastard, that's it, sleep away, let's get those shoes off your feet. I'm going to need those later. They're part of my plan.'

He suddenly shifted his position, farting loudly, and for one awful moment she thought he may have heard her speaking out, elucidating her internal dialogue like she'd never dared before. But no, he was close to unconsciousness, breathing deeply with a thin stream of saliva drooling from his open mouth, running down his stubbled chin towards his neck.

Kathy reached out tentatively and shook her husband, but he didn't stir. She shook him again, more vigorously this time, using all her limited strength and weight to move his body backwards and forwards, but he slept on oblivious to her activities. Kathy released her fragile grip, smiling as her confidence suddenly soared.

'Are you sleeping, monster man? Are you at my mercy for the first time in your sad life? I think so. I really do think so. You're lying there, drugged, snoring, totally unaware of my intentions. You're not in control anymore. You seem vulnerable enough to me.'

Kathy checked her pocket for the empty tablet bottle, holding it tightly in one hand before dropping it to the floor. This was it. The time had come. Now all she had to do was implement the rest of her plan without a single error. There was no room for mistakes. Everything had to be perfect. Nothing less was acceptable. He'd taught her that. Now to take full advantage.

Kathy hurried downstairs two steps at a time, empowered by her early success, adrenalin surging through her system, driving her on. Get the bags from the shed. That was next. Put on the surgical gloves and bring a hammer. Come on, Kathy, you can do it, girl. She'd started, and she'd finish too.

Kathy turned up the radio's volume to maximum, flooding the house with reassuringly loud rock music, before heading back upstairs. She left everything she was going to need on the landing, well out of the way but easily accessible when required. Yes, yes, that was best. That made sense. She was nothing if not organised. And everything was progressing even better than she'd hoped. She just had to keep going.

Kathy took the hammer in her gloved hand and began pounding away at the bathroom door until the wooden panel directly above the lock was cracked, splintered and fatally weakened to such an extent that she could see through to the other side. That's it, Kathy, that's it, bang, bang, bang, harder and harder, almost done.

She reached through the resulting hole when the hammer finally broke through, confirming that she could reach the internal lock before opening the door. Get the bastard's fingerprints on the hammer's grip. That was the next job. She couldn't forget a single thing. Not if she were to make it stick.

Kathy crossed the landing and placed the heavy steel hammer's rubber-covered shaft in her husband's open hand, closing his fingers around it, ensuring each digit made contact with the rubber, and then letting it fall to the floor. Best pop back downstairs and put the radio off. The noisy bit was over, done and dusted. There was no point in inviting attention from interfering neighbours. Not when the distraction was no longer required. She had to get a knife anyway. It was a win-win situation. Everything was progressing perfectly.

Kathy returned back upstairs, standing on the small landing, appreciating the silence for a few seconds more before stripping herself naked. She put her clothes to one side, in a corner well out of the way, threw the filleting knife across the landing onto the bedroom floor with a flick of her wrist, and entered the bathroom with the first bag of blood held tightly in one hand. She noticed that she'd stopped trembling for the first time in months as she opened it carefully, smothering the scarlet liquid all over her body. Kathy lowered herself to the floor and began rolling on the linoleum for a minute or two until finally satisfied with her efforts. Next, she manoeuvred herself across the landing towards the top of the stairs, all the time remaining on her back and pushing herself along with jerky movements that left her very close to exhaustion. She encouraged herself on as her body flagged. Come on, Kathy, you can do it, girl. Keep going, keep going. It will all be worth it in the end.

Kathy inhaled deeply, sucking in the air and exploding it from her lungs, before picking up her husband's highly polished black leather shoes from where she'd left them next to the bannister. She put them on her feet, first one and then the other, tying the laces as tightly as possible. They were too big of course, far too big, just as she'd anticipated with her much smaller feet. But they'd have to do. They served a necessary purpose. That's what mattered. They were an essential part of the plan.

Kathy struggled in the direction of the bathroom and flung the remainder of the first bag of blood all over the room, covering as much of the lower surfaces as possible. She then took the second bag, pouring the entire contents over the carpeted floor immediately outside the bathroom door, so that it soaked the required area. Kathy looked down, smiled emptily without parting her lips and walked back to the bedroom, leaving visible size-eleven bloody footprints as she went. She opened the third bag and poured most of the contents over Michael Conner's sleeping body, ensuring to cover both his hands and arms right up to the elbow in the process. As a final touch, she retrieved the sharp knife and empty brown plastic medicine bottle from the floor, covered each in blood, and then pressed each in turn into his open right hand, ensuring his fingers made contact with the relevant surfaces, leaving the desired prints in the correct places.

Kathy approached the bedroom door, satisfied with her progress, looking back at her unconscious husband, the man who had brought so much unbridled misery into her life, and she truly believed that she may finally escape him. He didn't seem nearly so powerful now, not so frightening or intimidating as he lay there, eyes open, staring into the unseen distance but seeing nothing at all. Kathy didn't see a terrifying monster anymore. Just the nasty little inadequate lowlife bully that he so obviously was. She resisted a sudden impulse to pick up the hammer and cave in his skull there and then where he lay. To beat him mercilessly until he breathed his last breath, or take hold of the razor-sharp knife and cut off his balls. It would feel *so* good to castrate the bastard. So very good to vent her pent-up rage! But what would that achieve? Nothing, once the initial euphoria had faded. There would be an inevitable price to pay. Imprisonment, incarceration for however long a court thought appropriate. It was almost a price worth paying to make him suffer as she had. But what about her baby? What about her child? Keep control, Kathy, keep control and resist the temptation. Implement the plan precisely as intended, to the letter and nothing more. That was the best. Prison wasn't an option, not for her, whatever he deserved. There was no room for murder, like it or not. She had to let the bastard live.

Kathy left the blood-drenched bedroom without looking back, placing the three empty bags in an orange supermarket carrier bag for later disposal. She opened the final pack of blood as she walked across the landing, down the stairs, through the hall, followed by the dining room and finally the kitchen, trailing blood as she went. By the time she opened the back door, walking out into the cold, semi-darkness of the evening, the final bag was almost empty, with only a few remaining drops left at the bottom. Kathy held up the bag at eye level and smiled. There was just enough to dribble across the concrete path to the edge of the lawn. She'd timed it to perfection. That's what she told herself. Who was useless now? Not her, definitely not her! She was the victor, a heroine, a lioness, a triumphant survivor at the very peak of her powers. The monster man's dominance was at an end. His bullying days were well and truly over. Here was hoping it stayed that way.

Kathy returned upstairs, repeating the entire journey on her bare bottom, sliding through the blood as she went, and effectively creating the convincing impression of a dead body being dragged through the house and towards the back garden. The results were even better than she could have hoped and, she decided, well worth the additional physical effort on her part. Every detail mattered. The murder scene had to be totally convincing whatever questions the police asked themselves. And they would. They definitely would.

Kathy washed at the kitchen sink, removing any sign of blood from her flagging body, paying particular attention to areas of skin that wouldn't be covered by clothes. Once satisfied with her efforts, she dried herself with a tea towel decorated with a stereotypical Christmas scene, throwing it into the carrier bag along with everything else for later disposal. It was time to head back upstairs once more. Time to throw the shoes onto the bedroom floor. Time to get dressed. Almost time to leave the house for the very last time. Almost time to abandon the obnoxious bastard to his fate. Hang on in there, Kathy. You've almost done it, girl. Just keep going and stick to the plan. That's all she had to do. Just hold her nerve and stick to the plan.

Kathy was careful not to step in any of the slowly congealing blood as she came back downstairs, fully dressed to the nines. She looked in the hall mirror for a moment and grinned on witnessing her reflection. She looked so very different from the woman she knew so well. The bright-blonde hair, heavy make-up and dark sculpted eyebrows were a triumph. As were plastic framed glasses with their non-prescription tinted lenses, which he'd sometimes used for his computer work when it suited him. They were, perhaps, a little large for her delicate features, a little manly possibly, but they certainly served their purpose well enough. Either way, they would have to do.

Kathy was filled with a new sense of calm confidence that grew exponentially as she lowered her gaze, walking on by. The disguise was almost perfect. She really couldn't have done any better. Even her closest relatives would struggle to recognise her at first sight. She really was going to escape and triumph. Everything was going her way. She was on the winning side for once, and he destined to lose. No mistakes, now all she had to do was keep it that way.

Kathy glanced nervously in every direction as she left the house for what she hoped was the very last time. She half expected to be caught out almost immediately. To be captured by some unknown adversary who'd drag her back, returning her to her husband's clutches, as if she'd never left. But to her relief, there was no one to see. No prying eyes looking to catch her out, no spies, if such people even existed outside her husband's head. The world seemed oblivious to her existence and that, she decided, was just fine with her. She picked up her pace, staying in the shadows, avoiding every street lamp, the orange sodium glow of which seemed brighter than she remembered. Almost like spotlights in a prison camp or on a Broadway stage. Kathy had absolutely no idea of her final destination as she strode purposefully in the direction of the railway station a mile or so away on the other side of the city, but anywhere else was preferable. She repeated it in her head. It really didn't matter where she ended up, as long as it was far away, where nobody recognised her or cared who she was. She just had to get on a train and go. To travel in continued hope and expectation. It wouldn't be easy. There would be trials. There were always trials. But what did it matter? He wouldn't be there. That was the crucial factor. She'd be free of his attention. Anywhere, absolutely anywhere, was better than being with him.

Intermittent rain began to fall from a dark and leaden sky as Kathy entered a red-painted phone box almost directly opposite the station's main entrance. She took a deep breath to steady herself, sucking in the cold night-time air and counting slowly to five, calming her jangling nerves before dialling 999 and waiting for a response that came almost immediately.

'Hello, caller, which emergency service do you require?'

'Police, please.'

'Hold on, caller. I'll put you through.'

'Devon and Cornwall Police, how can we help you?'

Kathy paused, shifting her weight from one foot to the other. This had better be good. It had to be convincing.

'How can I assist you, caller?'

Kathy responded in a well-practised southern Irish brogue, very different to her usual accent. 'I thought I heard a woman screamin' when I walked past forty-two Moonlight Drive 'bout an hour ago. She sounded as if she was in one helluva a state. Totally terrified so she was. I haven't been able to stop thinking about it ever since. I should have rung sooner. I wish I had now. I didn't want to get involved.'

'Did the sound of screaming come from *inside* the house or *outside* of the house?'

'It came from inside, definitely inside. I've no doubt at all.'

'And you say this happened about an hour ago?'

'Yes, that's correct. That's what I said.'

'Can you be more specific, give me an exact time?'

'Um, no, sorry, not really, I didn't look at me watch. An hour is an estimate rather than a statement of fact. I didn't mean to mislead you. That's the last thing I'd want.'

'Okay, caller, I understand. What's your full name and address, please?'

Kathy put the phone down. She pushed the heavy door open with new-found energy she hadn't known existed, fastened the top button of her scarlet coat against the cold and headed towards the ticket office, a beaming smile on her face. Now all she had to do was get on a train to God only knew where, create a new identity and get on with her life as best she could. She was finally free of her tormentor. Her world was a better place. A happier place, soon to be free of fear. Kathy pictured her husband's boyish face in her mind's eye and spat her words, addressing him as if he was there to listen but posed no threat at all.

'Goodbye, you vicious bastard, goodbye forever! You're going to get exactly what you deserve. You made my life a misery, and now it's your turn. You're going to suffer as I did. My new life is about to begin.'

Kathy patted her belly gently and smiled contentedly as the unmistakable noise of a siren sounded in the far distance before suddenly fading away to silence. She talked as she walked, whispering her words in soft reassuring tones, almost like a lullaby.

'We're going to have a nice life together, baby, so much fun. Just you and I make two. Let's pretend the last few years never happened. Let's make out as if I never met the bully boy with his deviant needs and abhorrent behaviour. You never knew him, and we'll keep it that way. Let's say that your father was someone else entirely, someone nice, someone of whose memory you can be proud. A soldier, maybe, or a sailor, someone who died a hero before you were born. We are going to be so very happy together. Just you wait and see. I'll make certain of it. I'm going to protect you and never let you down. If hell can be a place on earth, then so can heaven.'

Chapter 13

Kathy boarded the first available train, waiting hidden on the platform for about twenty minutes before her journey to liberty continued. She found a seat in a quiet carriage at the furthest point from the buffet car, having told herself insistently that fewer fellow passengers were likely to pass by, with the reduced risk that entailed. Kathy was still confident in her disguise. She'd thought it through, planned it in detail and executed it to the very best of her ability. But the fewer people who saw her, the better. That's what she told herself. Mike would have been found by now, whether unconscious or drowsy. Police activity would likely be frantic. It seemed obvious. It made absolute sense. All that blood and her nowhere to be found. They'd be looking for a body, her body. She had to stay off the radar, anonymous, incognito, hidden in plain sight. Being recognised would ruin everything.

Kathy closed her tired eyes and slowly drifted into a fitful sleep, her head vibrating against the glass as the throbbing diesel engine sped the train's six carriages through the dark West Country countryside towards Bristol Temple Meads Railway Station – an approximate two-hour journey away. She was dreaming again now, emotionally resonant, wild, imaginary images and sounds playing in her head like a dramatic horror film she was forced to both watch and experience. Mike had woken prematurely from the effects of her drug-induced cosh and had read her thoughts. He was chasing her, hunting her down and getting nearer with every second that passed, murderous intentions at the forefront of his mind. She kept running, but not nearly fast enough, as her legs weakened and threatened to fail. Mike was gaining on her, his face contorting, spewing hate. And then she tripped, fell, and he was looming over her, as he had many times in life, with a clenched fist raised high above his head. She screamed as Mike reached down, clutching her throat and squeezing as she pressed herself hard against the ground.

For one brief awful moment Kathy thought her dream had become a grim reality when shaken awake by the uniformed ticket inspector on reaching her intended destination. She stared up at him with wide, haunted eyes that gradually relaxed as her dream faded and reality dawned. She sighed and settled. It was just a dream, a nightmare, the creation of her subconscious mind, nothing more than that.

'Sorry to wake you, love. We've reached Bristol.'

Kathy thanked him in a trembling whisper, rising to her feet, half expecting her husband to suddenly appear and drag her back to her prison home as if she'd never left. She glanced to the right and left with quick furtive movements of her head on stepping into the aisle, but as she looked out on the bright lights shining in nearby buildings, she instinctively decided to continue her journey. Why not travel on to Newport, Cardiff, Swansea and beyond? The further she went from her home city, the better... why not stay on the train? It seemed so clear, so logical as if staring her in the face. Every mile she journeyed was to her advantage, a potential bonus that shouldn't be ignored. And rural West Wales seemed the perfect choice for her new life, with its modest population, remote villages and rolling green hills that kissed the sea. It seemed so right. Why hadn't she thought of it before?

Kathy bought a new one-way ticket for cash, returned to her seat, turned towards the window and closed her eyes again. She travelled back in time but to a happy place this time, a place that made her smile. She recalled childhood holidays on the beautiful Pembrokeshire coast, where she'd spent happy, carefree, sun-drenched summer days playing with Anna on soft sandy pale-yellow beaches, busy with happy holidaymakers that seemed to feel as joyous as she did as they went about their day. And then her father's voice in her ear with his arm around her sister's shoulder. As if he hadn't left them. As if he hadn't died.

'Do you two fancy an ice-cream before heading back to the caravan? Ninety-nines if you like? Sprinkles too, if you're lucky.'

Kathy found strength in the memories that moved and surprised her. She beamed as the past reached out, telling herself that she could replicate those happy times for her own child if all went well. If she didn't deviate from her plan even for a single second. She was feeling slightly more relaxed now, more positive, a faint but discernible light shining at the end of a long, dark tunnel of oppression. But as another passenger boarded the train, sitting opposite her, Kathy slowly opened her eyes. She was instantly back in the present, on full alert, her happy thoughts brought to an unanticipated halt as her knees knocked and her hands shook.

Kathy felt a growing sense of panic rise from her stomach and settle in her throat. She looked away, focussing on the window as opposed to the carriage, as the passenger settled in her seat. And then the woman spoke. She actually spoke. And Kathy feared her plan may be unravelling there and then before it had really begun.

'I hope you don't mind me asking. Do we know each other? I'm sure I recognise you from somewhere.'

Kathy glanced at the woman and then quickly looked away, turning her entire head rather than just her eyes. Was fate toying with her? Was some great puppet master in the sky paying games with her sanity? Kathy studied the woman's reflection in the glass, taking it in. Surely she'd remember that face? The pale, seemingly translucent skin, the coal-black hair and amber eyes. She was striking, beautiful and hard to forget. The sort of woman who stuck in your mind. Kathy briefly considered rising to her feet and hurrying to another carriage entirely, in the hope that her own unremarkable features were far less memorable, but she could feel the woman's eyes on her and decided she had to break the pervasive silence.

'No, I don't think so.'

And then the woman spoke again as Kathy sat there statue-like, frozen in indecision, wishing the floor would open and swallow her whole.

'I'm sure we were at university together. Your hair is different now, and you didn't wear glasses in those days, but I'm certain I recognise your face. We were in the same year. I've got a good memory for that sort of thing.'

Kathy clenched her jaw.

'No, as I said, you're mistaken.'

'I was studying Law, and you were on another degree course on the same campus. We chatted once in the student's union bar after a few drinks. There was a punk band playing live. I think it may have been freshers' week... Anna, that's it, Anna something or other! You have the same name as my mother. Talking to you reminded me of home.'

Kathy shifted her weight from one buttock to the other, weighing up her limited options. What to say? What on earth to say? Think, Kathy, think... she had to say something. Silence wasn't an option. Not if she was going to get away.

'I didn't go to university. I didn't get the A level grades I needed. Such a disappointment, but that's the way it was.'

The woman pulled her head back, seemingly studying Kathy's features, refusing to look away.

'Really, I could swear I recognise you? I've got a virtually photographic recall for faces. I rarely get these things wrong.'

Kathy glared at her, eyes flashing.

'Well, you're wrong on this occasion. My name's not Anna, and I didn't attend your university or any other for that matter. Now, leave it there, please. You're thinking of someone else entirely. I don't know who, but it certainly wasn't me.'

'Sorry, I was just making conversation. I didn't mean to cause any offence. If I've made an error, I can only apologise.'

Kathy adopted a more conciliatory tone.

'It's not a problem, I'm tired, that's all. I've had a long day. I need to sleep.'

'I really am sorry. I won't bother you again.'

Kathy closed her eyes and kept them tight shut, counting the seconds until the woman finally left the train at Cardiff's busy city centre station. She watched as the woman walked along the platform with its view of the impressive rugby stadium standing proudly on the banks of the Taff, and said a silent prayer, more in hope than expectation, as the woman disappeared from sight.

'Please, God, keep us both safe.'

Maybe she'd gotten away with it. Perhaps she'd said enough to protect her anonymity. Maybe the woman had forgotten her already. Kathy linked her hands in front of her, still deep in melancholy thought. Hopefully, the cruel attentions of fate had passed her by.

Kathy rushed towards the nearest toilet as the train continued its journey west a few minutes later, locking herself in the cubicle with her arms folded tightly across her body until she finally heard the announcer speak out their arrival in the small Welsh market town of Caerystwyth about an hour and a half later. She opened the toilet door, just a few inches at first, peeping out between door and frame and watching the remaining passengers disembark one after another, right up to the time she thought the situation best minimised the risks to her advantage. Kathy jumped from the train with her coat collar high as the final fellow passenger left her sight. She looked into but chose not to enter a brightly lit waiting room to escape the cold, opting instead to sit in the darkest corner of the station platform to wait for morning. Kathy drifted in and out of broken sleep as the hours slowly passed, shivering uncontrollably, teeth chattering as the December temperature dropped a degree or two below zero. She stood and stamped both feet in a hopeless attempt to ward off the cold as dawn slowly approached, wishing the minutes away until the sun finally rose on the far horizon and the sky softened.

A thin mist rose from the river shrouding the surrounding fields at chest level as Kathy walked into town at just after 7am that morning, keen to find a suitably cheap hotel or guest house where she could warm herself and rest.

She strode along the frosty pavement, breaking into a quick loping trot more than once, keen to avoid the potential attention of any passer-by or early morning drivers starting their day. Kathy quickly rejected the only hotel she came to, thinking the three-star establishment too expensive for her limited finances.

She trudged on with an increasingly heavy heart as a light flurry of tiny snowflakes began to swirl at the behest of a strengthening east wind and stung her face. She was starting to question if she'd ever find somewhere even remotely suitable as her resolve weakened, but within half an hour she'd spotted a backstreet pub with a faded, yellowed poster advertising an available room pasted to one of its grimy ground floor windows. Kathy stood on the gradually whitening pavement, looking at the building less than enthusiastically for a few seconds before finally deciding that anywhere was better than trudging the streets in the cold light of day. She tried the door, which was locked, and then began knocking with the knuckles of one hand, softly at first – fearing her husband may open it and drag her in – but then firmer with gradually increasing energy as she drove her irrational thoughts from her mind. Kathy looked up nervously, shielding her face from the falling snow as a first-floor window opened, and a middle-aged man with a balding head and gunmetal glasses called out to her in agitated tones that made her wince.

'What do you want, love? It's not even eight yet. I had a late night.'

Kathy briefly considered walking away without a response, but she glanced down at her blue numb hands and decided to stand her ground.

'I saw your advert in the window. The room for rent, I'd like to stay if it's still available.'

He looked her up and down, slowly, studying the line of her full breasts under her scarlet coat.

'It's forty quid a night. And I only take cash in advance, no cards and no exceptions. No even for a pretty young thing like you.'

Kathy transferred her weight from one foot to the other, looking away at nothing in particular as he continued to stare.

'Cash is fine with me. That's not going to be an issue.'

'Right, don't you move an inch. A quick bathroom visit to splash the porcelain and I'll be with you before you know it. Just you hold on there.'

Kathy stood shivering on the wintry pavement as the landlord disappeared from sight, repeatedly reminding herself that as seedy and rundown as the establishment so obviously was, with its less than charming host, anywhere was preferable to being with her husband. She repeated it in her mind as the sky grew darker and cast its shadows. She needed rest. She needed shelter. And anywhere was better than home.

Kathy was lost in thought, travelling back in time to a black and oppressive place, when the door suddenly opened with a strangely disconcerting groan that made her flinch. The landlord was standing there in the entrance, dressed in nothing but a pair of navy-blue boxer shorts and an inadequately sized white cotton T-shirt stretched to maximum over his protruding beer belly. He had a smouldering cigarette hanging from the right-hand corner of a mouth dominated by uneven nicotine-yellowed teeth that Kathy silently observed looked even more unkempt than the rest of him.

The landlord focussed on Kathy, holding her gaze right up to the moment she lowered her head.

When he eventually spoke, it was with a hoarse, phlegmy smoker's rattle that Kathy found challenging to decipher.

'In you come, love. Come on, get out of the cold. It's brass monkeys out there. The weatherman on the telly said it's coming straight from Siberia.'

He took two backward steps, moving aside to allow Kathy to enter a dingy, dimly lit room, seemingly filled with faded brown furniture that had long since seen better days. There was a worn out dart board on one white-painted wall, and a little jukebox with an out of order sign stuck on the front of another. Every conceivable surface was littered with dirty glasses and drink-sodden beer mats. Kathy took repeated shallow breaths, thinking the room stunk of ale and stale tobacco despite the smoking ban.

The man took the fag from his mouth, flicking orange ash onto the bare wooden floorboards.

'Sorry 'bout the mess. We had a darts match last night. We're top of the league. A few of the lads stayed for a lock-in.'

Kathy didn't reply.

'Do you want to see the room before paying? People often do for some reason. It's not five-star, but it's comfortable enough.'

She thought about it for a few seconds but decided against.

'No, it's all right, thank you, I'll only be staying for a night or two, and I need to rest. If we can sort out the money, I'll go straight up.'

He placed his hands on his fleshy hips, leaning back slightly and frowning.

'Which is it, love, one night or two? Like I said, it's cash up front. You need to make your mind up. I hope you're not going to mess me about.'

'You said it's forty pounds a night, yes?'

The landlord briefly considered increasing the price, but he noted Kathy's lack of luggage, changing his mind at the last moment.

'Yeah, that's for bed and board, but you'll have to sort out your own breakfast. My missus is visiting her mother up north. There's no one to do the cooking. You can help yourself if you want to or there's a caff on the corner if that suits you better.' He pointed to his left. 'That's the door to the kitchen. It's up to you. I try to avoid the place whenever possible. It's a matter of principle.'

Kathy turned away, counting out eight ten-pound notes, before handing them to him without the need for words.

He crossed the floor, reached behind the bar and handed her a door key attached to a large wooden fob with the number two written on it in felt pen.

'The room's at the top of the stairs, second door on the right. There's a shared bathroom opposite. There's just you and me at the moment so you won't be disturbed. Make yourself at home. It's a friendly pub. You'll like the locals if you get the chance to meet them.'

Kathy smiled and nodded. 'I'll go on up then.'

'You do that, love. I need to sort this place out.' He pointed in the direction of the cluttered bar. 'Look at the state it's in.'

Kathy was met by the unmistakable dank odour of chronic damp as she entered the small box room with its single bed, free-standing Victorian wardrobe and wooden chair. She thought she heard a faint scuttling sound coming from above the ceiling as she locked the door with a single turn of the key, wedging the high back of the chair under the door's discoloured brass handle in the interests of security. She shuddered as she turned away, glancing into the grey-white street before closing the yellow curtains and slumping onto the lumpy, overly firm mattress, choosing to rest fully clothed on top of the bedclothes rather than climb under the thin quilt.

Kathy lay back, staring at the ceiling with unblinking eyes, and hoping that the noise of tiny clawed feet indicated mice as opposed to rats. She looked to each corner of the room, taking it all in for the first time. It was the least aesthetically pleasing space she'd ever entered, let alone stayed in. There was no doubt on that score. But so what? What did it matter? Her husband wasn't there. That's what counted. She repeated it in her head. She was safe. Her unborn child was safe. The monster man wouldn't suddenly appear with his criticisms, threats or worse. There would no punches or kicks to bruise her vulnerable flesh. No cruel blows placing her baby's life in danger as before. Perhaps she'd never see the bastard's hateful face again, except in her flashbacks and nightmares. Maybe she really had escaped him this time. Perhaps she'd already won.

Kathy closed her tired eyes and tried to relax, picturing a black velvet hammock in a pitch-black room filled with unconditional love. By the time she finally drifted into sporadic sleep, forty minutes had passed and she woke several times in the coming hours, eventually rising to the sound of drunken singing at ten past one that afternoon.

She stood, stretched, picked up her coat, and made a brief but necessary bathroom visit, splashing her face with ice cold water to help shake off the residual elements of sleep. Kathy stared into the oval mirror above the white porcelain sink and decided she looked exhausted and drained yet somehow happy. There was less tension in her face. No fear in her eyes. Or at least none that she was willing to acknowledge. What would that achieve? Now wasn't the time for doubts or indecision. She had to stay strong.

There were three male customers in the dimly lit bar when Kathy entered the room, in addition to the landlord, who was in the process of serving a pint of strong German lager to a grossly overweight, red-faced drunk in a poorly fitting business suit. She glanced at each man in turn, weighing them up, trying to read their thoughts before lowering her eyes as the landlord called out to her with the hint of a smile playing on his pudgy face.

'Nice to see you up and about, love. Are you going to take your coat off and have a drink with your new friends? We could do with a bit of female company. The first ones on the house, my treat.'

Kathy fastened her coat as she approached the bar, struggling with the top button as her hands began to shake.

'No thanks, but maybe tonight or sometime tomorrow. It's kind of you to offer, but there are things I need to do. Things I can't afford to delay. I need to get on.'

The landlord began pouring the drunk another pint as she stood to wait.

'Okay, love, anything you say. Have it your way. But if you change your mind, just say the word. I'm at your service, your jovial host.'

Kathy cleared her throat.

'Do you happen to know if there's a social services office here in town?'

'Do you mean the benefits place?'

Kathy shook her head as one of two elderly domino players began blasting out an inept rendition of an old Welsh hymn she didn't recognise or appreciate. She rested her elbows on the bar, craned her neck, and spoke up above the noise.

'No, *social services*, not social security, I need to speak to a social worker.'

He looked back at her with a blank expression.

'Are you sure you won't have a drink, love? You look as if you could do with one. On the house, as I said. You could do with a bit of cheering up, no charge.'

'No, I'd better make a move. Things to do, people to see. But thanks anyway. You're very kind.'

Kathy was about to approach the exit when the overweight drunk burped loudly. He tapped her on the shoulder, placing her on full alert as dark memories flooded back and threatened to swamp her.

'It's in Glyndwr Street, upstairs, opposite the off-licence.' He pointed at his leg. 'I used to work there before the accident.'

Kathy's eyes widened.

'You worked for social services?'

'Yeah, admin, I was there for about ten years all told. I lost my leg in a motorcycle accident. It was all downhill after that; far too much morphine. You get used to the stuff, that's the problem. It becomes less effective with time.'

'I'm sorry.'

He took a generous slurp of lager, wiping his mouth with a soiled sleeve.

'Life's not fair, sod's law, no one said it was.'

'Does the local office deal with childcare issues?'

He nodded twice with a barely noticeable movement of his massive head, emptying his glass with one smooth gulp.

'Just ask for the duty social worker. If they can help you, they will. And tell them Joey said hello.' He tapped his false leg with a rat-tat-tat. 'They're not a bad bunch all considered. I haven't seen any of them for ages.'

Chapter 14

Kathy sat, cross-legged, in the social services waiting room, reading one remarkably similar women's magazine after another, until a slim young man with shoulder-length chestnut-brown hair, a well-trimmed beard and round gold-metal framed glasses finally put his head around the door and called out, 'Who's next?'

Kathy noted the social worker's kindly eyes as she rose to her feet and followed him into a small, cluttered interview room on the opposite side of the corridor.

He reached out and shook her hand before closing the door. 'My name's John, John Hardy, I'm the duty officer for today. Take a seat and tell me how I can help you.'

Kathy took off her woollen coat, hung it on the back of the chair and sat as instructed. Hardy took a seat opposite her with an open referral pad perched on his lap.

Kathy looked at him, taking comfort in those gentle eyes, blurting out her words like a torrent of sound she couldn't hope to stop even if she wanted to. She wanted him to know everything, every little detail. But she had to select her words with caution. Some things weren't for sharing.

'I'm pregnant, my husband's violent towards me, he'll kill the child if he gets even the slightest opportunity. That's the sort of man he is. Evil personified! We need your help to stay safe.' Yes, keep it simple, that was best. Just outline the facts and leave it at that.

The social worker jerked his head back, struck by the raw emotional intensity of her statement.

'Do you *really* think he'd do that?'

'Oh, *yes*, I've already suffered one miscarriage due to his violence. He hit me in the gut and laughed as he did it. It was deliberate, planned, he knew exactly what he was doing. The bastard hasn't got a caring bone in his body. Sadism defines him.'

Hardy's brow furrowed. As if it mattered. As if it was more than a job. As if he genuinely wanted to help.

'Okay, you've come to the right place. Let's start with your name and address.'

Kathy paused, brushing non-existent fluff from a sleeve. A false identity was crucial. Anonymity was everything.

'It's, er, it's Hazel, Hazel Goddard. I've travelled here from London. Near Greenwich. A nice part of the city.'

'What was your address, please, Hazel?'

She avoided his gaze. Why did she say so much? Stupid! Why add unnecessary detail? 'Um… I'm sorry, I er, I don't want to give it.'

He poised his pen above the referral form.

'Okay, we can take this one step at a time if that makes you feel better. Have you spoken to the police either here or in London?'

Kathy visibly stiffened.

'No, I don't want the police involved, please, no police, that's *really* important to me. If my husband gets even the *slightest* clue where I am, he'll come after me whatever the law says or does. It wouldn't be the first time. I've tried and failed to get away several times over the years. He'd come after me and drag me back. I can't let that happen again.' She placed an open hand on her abdomen. 'Not now, not when there's another life to consider.'

'I'm going to have to discuss your situation with the local police child protection team at some point in the not too distant future. It's a joint process. It's not something I can avoid given your circumstances.'

Kathy stood, a look of escalating panic etched on her face as she considered bolting for the door.

'Please sit back down, Hazel, no one can make you provide any information you want to keep to yourself, not me, and not the police. Tell us *exactly* what you want to tell us and no more. It's your prerogative. You're in control.'

She slumped back in her seat, exhaling the air from her mouth with an audible hiss.

'Thank you, that means a lot.'

He smiled, keen to help her relax.

'How long have you been here in town?'

'Since yesterday morning.'

'So, where did you stay last night?'

Kathy's eyes blinked like a faulty bulb.

'The Golden Pheasant, I think it's called. It's a bit of a dump but I was glad to get out of the cold.'

He grimaced.

'Yeah, I know it.'

'I need to find something cheaper until I can afford a place of my own. I don't care where, just as long as there aren't too many questions. It's a new start. I want to focus on that.'

'Okay, I get where you're coming from. What's your financial position? Let's talk about the practicalities.'

Kathy patted a pocket.

'I've got about three hundred quid to my name. I'm hoping to get some form of benefit until I find work. I've never claimed anything in my life. I guess now's the time to start.'

He nodded.

'Okay, that all makes sense. Do you fancy a coffee while I make some calls?'

Kathy's eyes narrowed, facial muscles taut.

'Not the police?'

'No, we can worry about them when the time's right. Now, how about that coffee? I'm making one anyway. It's no bother.'

Kathy grinned, silently acknowledging that she was taking a liking to the good-looking man with his kindly eyes and generous disposition.

'That would be lovely, thank you.'

'How do you take it?'

'Milk no sugar.'

'I'll be back with you in five minutes.'

Kathy accepted her mug, cupping her hands around it to warm them, as the social worker left the room for a second time. She sat and waited, tapping a foot on the floor until he returned minutes later. When he spoke his tone was upbeat, his face expressive, exuding optimism as if things weren't so bad after all.

'Right, I've got some good news for you. One of my clients is leaving the women's refuge here in town the day after tomorrow. I've had a word with the powers that be and the room's yours for as long as you need it. What do you think? Rooms don't become available all that often. The timing's rather fortuitous if you're in agreement.'

Kathy looked at him with a pensive expression.

'That's the last thing I was expecting.'

'What do you think? I'd give it serious consideration if I were you. I don't think there's any downsides, except for those few people who can't cope with the communal living.'

'I can't see that being a problem for me.'

'So, you're saying yes?'

'Um, yeah, I can't see why not, thank you.'

'That's it, best stay positive, look on the bright side.' He reached into the inside pocket of his corduroy jacket, handing her a white card with the refuge's address and contact number printed on the front in blue ink. 'Keep that information as confidential as you can. The fewer people who know the location, the better. You know, for obvious reasons. I'm sure I don't need to explain.'

Kathy glanced at the card and nodded. 'I will.'

He crossed his legs. 'What sort of employment have you got in mind?'

'Um… perhaps shop work or waitressing, something along those lines. I haven't got the experience for much else. My husband made sure of that. I just hope I've got the confidence to do anything at all.'

'He made sure how?'

Kathy's expression darkened.

'Working was out of the question. I might have said something to the wrong person.'

Hardy sighed. 'That sounds all too familiar. Far too many women suffer at the hands of inadequate bullies.'

The skin bunched around Kathy's eyes in a pained stare as she pictured Conner hovering over her, spitting spite, oozing malice.

'I hope I never set eyes on the vile bastard again.'

'You did the right thing getting out when you did.'

Kathy nodded her enthusiastic agreement, leaning forwards in her seat with her hands on her knees.

'I still can't quite believe I'm free. I have to pinch myself to prove I'm not dreaming. That it's real. That I actually got away and escaped the vicious bastard. However tough things are from here on in, they are *never* going to be as bad as what I went through at his hands. It's like a dark cloud has finally lifted from my life. And things are going to get *even* better. I just know they are. It's my time now. Mine and my baby's.'

The social worker raised a hand to his face, massaging his chin between thumb and fingers.

'Did you really not see the type of man he was before you married him? Weren't there any clues? Did he hide it that well?'

'It's only now I'm starting to fully appreciate just how utterly controlling he was right from the very start of our relationship. I think I was still vulnerable after the death of my father when we first met. He must have seen that I was grieving and used it to his advantage. He played me to perfection.'

'Yeah, that all makes sense. Men like him hone in on any perceived weakness or vulnerability. That's how they operate.'

'That's *exactly* what he did. He's an exploiter, and he's good at it, one of the best. He taunted me and broke me down one day at a time for his own deviant pleasure. Like a cat playing with a mouse. What on earth's wrong with the man? Why would *anyone* behave like that?'

The social worker moved forward in his seat. 'I'm beginning to understand what you've been through. I've come across men like him before. It's something I have to deal with all too often in my line of work. Everything that happened was his responsibility. It's important to remember that. You're a survivor now. He's wherever he is, and you're here changing your life.'

Kathy smiled humourlessly. 'I'd love to have seen the look on his ugly face when he first realised I'd actually gone for good. I'm sure he thought he had me imprisoned forever, his property, that's what he used to say. I belonged to him, like a slave. He could do whatever he wanted and whenever he wanted without fear of consequence. I don't think he ever thought of me as a real person, certainly not an individual with the right to self-determination. He controlled my life and everything I did because it amused and pleased him to toy with my sanity. If I hadn't become pregnant for a second time, well, I'd still be there now, living a life of misery, dancing to his tune as he pulled my strings like some crazed puppet master teetering on the edge of insanity.' The contours of her face relaxed and she looked suddenly younger. 'But I'm not still there. I'm here talking to you. And that's my victory! I'm a survivor, just like you said. I'm not his victim anymore. I won in the end despite his perceived dominance. I won, and he lost.'

The social worker smiled thinly.

'You've done well. You should be extremely proud of yourself. Not everyone would have been able to leave as you did. It took real courage.'

Kathy touched her abdomen again with gentle affection, picturing the life inside her.

'I've got my baby to thank for that. We escaped the bastard together, and we're never going back. He's not used to losing, but he's lost this time. I hope that reality tears him apart one day at a time. That it eats away at him like a rabid dog and destroys him like he tried to destroy me. He deserves that after everything he did to me and to the child I lost. That's the price he has to pay.'

Hardy frowned, pondering the emotional strength of her declaration. 'He sounds like seriously bad news.'

'Oh yes, he is. I haven't told you the half of it.'

'I'm sorry you had to go through all that. It sounds almost too much to bear.'

Kathy averted her gaze to the wall. 'It was.'

'And you're sure you don't want to give me his name? He'd be arrested and prosecuted too if there's sufficient evidence to prove a case against him. He deserves that, doesn't he? After everything he's done. Don't you think he should face justice?'

Kathy picked at the skin of her wrist, eyes focussed on the floor. 'I can't go down that road.'

He paused, choosing his words carefully.

'Men like your husband don't change their behaviour unless they're made to stop. If not you, he'll move on to hurt somebody else. I hear what you're saying, but I'd like you to reconsider. The court system is there for a reason. It could be used to your advantage and that of others.'

Kathy jumped up in her seat, shaking her head frantically, eyes wide.

'No, no, no! That was *never* a part of my plan. I can't give evidence. Going back is not an option, not now, not *ever*. It's completely out of the question, unthinkable. I need you to understand and accept that. I've done *everything* I need to do to negate the danger he poses. Going back would ruin everything.'

'The department could help you apply for an injunction. I know an excellent female lawyer who specialises in exactly this kind of predicament.'

'No, no, you've said enough. I think I've made myself perfectly clear. I have to forget my husband and get on with my new life, for my own sake and the baby's too. If you can't agree to that, I'm getting out of here *now*. I thought you were here to help me, not to pressure me into doing something I don't want to do. I'm beginning to wish I hadn't come here at all.'

The social worker held up his hands as if surrendering, his palms forwards and open, his face flushed.

'Okay, I'm sorry, no one is going to make you do anything you don't want to do, least of all me. That's the last thing you need after everything you've been through. If you feel I've been overly assertive, I can only apologise. It wasn't my intention.'

Kathy relaxed slightly, unfolding her arms. 'Do you promise?'

'Absolutely, you have my word.'

Hardy made some quick notes before checking his watch and rising to his feet. 'Okay, we're done for now. It was very nice to meet you, circumstances apart. You'll be allocated a social worker who'll offer you support and advice as needed. That's inevitable given the potential risks to your unborn child. It'll probably be a couple of days before you hear from anybody, but you've got the refuge's address and contact details, so you can make the necessary arrangements for yourself. Ask for Sally Jones when you ring. I'll speak to her sometime later today and make sure she's expecting your call. Sally's the domestic violence support worker. You'll like her. She was one of the residents herself not so very long ago. She won't mind me telling you that. She's rightly proud of all she's achieved. And she'll understand exactly what you're going through. You couldn't be in better hands. Have you got a mobile number?'

'No, no, I haven't as yet.'

'No problem, we can contact you via the refuge.'

'Will it be you? The social worker, will it be you?'

'Um, that will be up to my team manager, but probably not. I've got a pretty busy caseload at the moment, and I've got a week's leave coming up after Christmas.'

Kathy fidgeted with her empty mug, revolving it in her hands, avoiding his gaze.

'I'd like it to be you, if at all possible. I'd rather not tell my story all over again. It's not something I find easy to do. It makes everything that happened all the more real somehow. It brings everything back. I hope that makes sense.'

He hesitated.

'I'll see what I can do, but no promises. Like I said, it's not my decision to make.'

Kathy stood to leave, fastening her coat one button at a time.

'Thank you so very much, it's appreciated. I really feel as if I'm winning. It's onwards and upwards from here on in. It's going to be as if my husband never existed. As if that was another life. I'm glad of your help. Hopefully, we'll meet again soon. I'd almost forgotten there's good men in the world as well as the bad.'

'Stay strong, Hazel. I'm glad you've found our discussion helpful. I like to think we good guys are in the majority. I hope we meet again too.'

Chapter 15

Police Inspector Michael Conner thought he must be experiencing a frightening and unpleasant dream when he first woke from his chemically induced slumber, with Hodgson sitting at his side with a dark and sullen expression dominating her otherwise attractive features. But as he narrowed his eyes against the bright electric glare shining down from above, and turned his aching head to the right and left, his new reality slowly dawned. He was in a hospital with a drip stand next to his bed, that was clear. But he had absolutely no idea why he was there or even what day it was. Unwelcome questions bombarded Conner's troubled intellect as he tried to make sense of the unfathomable. Questions he couldn't hope to answer. Questions that undermined his self-confidence, diminishing the feelings of superiority and infallibility that were usually at the forefront of his mind. His situation confused him. It unnerved him. But it was real. It was all too real.

Conner fought to regain his composure as his unfamiliar situation chipped away at his ego, threatening to reveal his true self to the world like never before. He took a deep breath through his nose, closing his eyes for a beat as he blew the air from his mouth. His mask was in danger of slipping, and he couldn't let that happen, not for a second. That would ruin everything. Such things were unthinkable. He had to play the game.

Hodgson rose from her chair, looking down at Conner with a contemptuous sneer she made no effort to hide.

'Good to have you back with us, inspector. It was touch and go for a while. The doctors tell me you very nearly died.'

He felt his entire body tense.

'What the hell are you talking about?'

'Oh come on, you know that as well as I do. Your attempted suicide. You tried to kill yourself. And you very nearly succeeded.'

His mouth fell open, eyes popping as his earlier confusion intensified. 'What, attempted suicide? No fucking way! I haven't heard anything so ridiculous in my life.'

Hodgson paused before responding, upping the pressure, noting the suppressed rage in his eyes, making him wait.

'You've been out of it for nearly forty-eight hours. If the doctors hadn't pumped your stomach, you'd have been a goner long before now. This was no cry for help. You meant it. You wanted to die. It was only a quirk of fate that saved you.'

Conner attempted to jump up in bed, to protest, to contradict her contention. But he fell back when his handcuffed left wrist jarred against the metal bed frame, making him wince. He pulled wildly at the cuffs, attempting and failing to free his arm and cutting his wrist in the process, dark blood running down his hand and staining the bedsheet one drop at a time.

'What the hell are these things all about? Get them unlocked. Get the fucking things off! Give me the key *now!*'

Hodgson didn't move an inch.

'Don't just sit there, woman. Get the fucking things off! I'm not a risk to myself. Get them off! And that's an order in case you were wondering. I'm still your superior. It might be an idea to remember that. Do what you're fucking told.'

'Oh, I don't think so, Mike. That's not going to happen. Your days of issuing orders are well and truly over.'

He clenched his jaw, growling, teeth bared, eyes narrowed to virtual slits as his blood pressure soared to a savage high.

'Have you gone insane, woman? What the fuck are you talking about? You're talking total shit.'

'I haven't seen this side of you before. The angry man. It's illuminating, to say the least. You were a good actor. I'll give you that much.'

'You'll get the fucking things off if you know what's good for you!'

Hodgson reached out, grabbing Conner's secured arm with a surprisingly firm grip.

'I'm arresting you on suspicion of murder. You do not have to say anything. But it may harm your defence if you do not mention when questioned, something that you later rely on in court. Anything you do say may be given in evidence. Is that clear enough for you? Or would you like me to repeat myself? You seem to be having problems grasping the gravity of your situation.'

Conner laughed coldly, spittle spraying from his open mouth as he glared at her, eyes flashing, wishing he could hit out and silence her forever.

'Is this a wind-up? Is there a hidden camera somewhere? It's a joke, right? This is a complete farce. It would be funny if it weren't so ridiculous. Who the fuck do you think I killed?'

'Oh, I think you know the answer to that.'

He was sweating now, chest puffed out, nostrils flared red, his breathing louder as his confused fury threatened to engulf him completely. 'You say I tried to kill somebody. You say I tried to kill *myself*. It's all crap! Total and utter shit. Now, get the cuffs off! I haven't done anything of the kind. It's all a fantasy of your own making. You're off your fucking head.'

'You're getting a little worked up, Mike. It might be an idea to shut your lying mouth until you've got a lawyer to hold your hand. I shouldn't need to tell you that. You're in enough trouble without making it even worse for yourself. You're not convincing anyone, not now, not anymore.'

Conner's head dropped, and for a fleeting moment she thought he may start weeping. He raised his eyes slowly a second later, speaking in a contrived more conciliatory tone he thought to his advantage, as he forced a scream back down his throat.

'What the hell are you talking about? I don't need a solicitor. Be reasonable, think about what you're saying. I'm a respected police inspector, not some lowlife offender. I really thought we were friends. We've known each other for a long time, remember?'

'I'm not playing your games.'

He looked incredulous, his mind darting from one unanswered question to the next as his gut twisted and spasmed.

'Games? I'm not playing games. What the hell's that supposed to mean?'

Hodgson moved to the end of his bed, in no hurry to explain, preparing to leave in her own time, when it suited her.

'You know how this works as well as I do. You'll be formally interviewed as soon as the doctors say you're fit for discharge. And don't even think about trying to escape justice. Even if you managed to get the cuffs off, which seems highly unlikely, there'll be a uniformed constable at the entrance to your room twenty-four hours a day for as long as you're here. You're not going anywhere.'

He held his unsecured hand out wide.

'Oh come on, Sarah, I thought we were mates. We work together. Have done for years. Have you forgotten who I am? This is crazy, totally fucking crazy! Think about what you're doing before it's too late. You're not doing your career any favours.'

Hodgson walked towards the door, stopping mid-step, looking back at him, feeling a heady mix of revulsion and regret.

'You had me conned. You had us all conned. We let Kathy down. I'll never forgive myself for that. I should have believed her. I should have acted on her allegations. Every word she said was true.'

'Kathy? Are you trying to say I murdered Kathy?'

'Why the denial? It's over. There's a price to pay for your crimes. Take responsibly for your actions. A confession would at least rescue your reputation to some extent. It's the one card you've got left to play.'

Conner began rocking back and forth in his bed, his eyes glazing over as he glared in her direction, thinking the world had gone mad.

'Now, you listen to me! I'm going to make myself crystal clear. I did not kill Kathy. I haven't touched the bitch. And there's not going to be a sentence. I'll be out of here and back in work before you know it. Get that into your thick head. I'm an innocent man.'

Hodgson suppressed a snigger.

'What is it with you, Mike, have you no shame? You made that poor woman's life a total misery, and then you took her life as if she didn't matter at all. She didn't deserve that. No woman deserves that. It's time to show some contrition. Let her family have her body for burial. Find some courage and face your guilt. Do the right thing for once in your life. Surely even you can see sense in that. The game's well and truly up.'

Conner began shouting now, his voice resonating with wild emotion as his chest tightened.

'You haven't found a body! What does that tell you? *Think*, woman! Stop making assumptions. Maybe then you'll see what's staring you in the face. Kathy's done a runner! She's not dead, she's gone. I have not touched her. Why aren't you listening to me? How many times do I have to say it? A trained chimp could work it out. It couldn't be more obvious if it were carved in tablets of fucking stone.'

Hodgson shook her head.

'Do you really think that I'm that stupid? Do you really think it's going to be that easy? The evidence speaks for itself. It tells an undeniable story. You're going to prison, Mike. You're going to be locked up. It's just a matter of how long for and what happens when you get there. Face facts and get used to it. The good times are over, whatever you say, whatever you do. I'm in control now. It's all downhill from here.'

Chapter 16

Kathy looked in one shop window after another, searching for non-existent written notifications of job vacancies, before finally building up sufficient courage to enter an independent women's clothes shop to enquire in person. She repeated the process without success for a little over an hour before eventually wandering into Merlin's Lane, a long and narrow walkway with small shops and occasional pubs, wine bars and restaurants on either side. She was about to give up on her quest and head for the job centre when a bright, bijou vegetarian cafe caught her eye no more than a two-minute walk from where she stood. Kathy checked her pockets for loose change as she walked towards the door, and glanced through the misted glass panes. There was something about the place she liked; a general vibe that pleased her. She pushed open the door, appreciating the comparative warmth that met her as she entered the airy room with its lilac paint, Christmas decorations, mistletoe, and original paintings by talented local artists festooning the walls. Kathy chose a two-seater black leather sofa near to the serving counter to sit in, took off her rain-sodden coat, and perused the menu for a minute or two before an attractive young waitress with striking pale-blue eyes and flame-red hair approached her table.

'Are you ready to order?'

Kathy looked up at the young woman's smiling face and felt immediately at ease. She looked a little like a childhood friend. A girl she'd liked immensely.

'Is it okay if I just have a bowl of soup?'

'Of *course* it is, no problem at all. We've got a nice chunky vegetable cawl or lentil and tomato.'

'Ooh, I think I'll have the cawl, it sounds delicious.'

The young woman noted the order on a small pad with a yellow pencil. 'Do you want bread with that?'

'Do you have gluten-free?'

The waitress nodded her head.

'One or two slices?'

'Two, please.'

'And some cheese?'

Kathy creased up her nose.

'No, not for me thanks. I'm lactose intolerant. My husband used to make me drink milk sometimes because it amused him.'

The young waitress frowned.

'That sounds terrible.'

'Yes, yes, it was.'

'Do you want anything else?'

'Just a glass of water, if that's okay? My throat is a bit sore. I think I may be going in for something.'

'Tap or bottled?'

'Just tap, please.'

The friendly waitress grinned for a second time before walking away with a sway of her hips.

'It'll be with you in five minutes.'

Kathy perused a colourful vegan recipe book taken from a packed bookcase with only limited interest as she sat and waited. She'd only reached page five by the time the waitress reappeared with a glass of water in one hand and a bowl of steaming cawl in the other. She placed both items on the table before fetching two slices of bread and a soup spoon seconds later.

'Enjoy! If there's anything else you need, just give me a shout. There's salt and pepper on the table.'

Kathy enjoyed the aromatic vapour rising from her bowl as she waited patiently for the cawl to cool. She spooned some from the very edge and blew it gently before swallowing. It was still a little too hot but very tasty; as good as any she could hope to make herself. She felt her jaw tense as she recalled the last time she'd prepared such a meal, but she relaxed slightly as she glanced around the room and drove the memory from her mind. That was the past and this was now. She had to live in the present. Take pleasure in the little things; the ordinary things that made life worthwhile.

Kathy dipped a half-slice of brown bread into her toothsome cawl and began eating with gusto. She was in a cafe and free to order whatever she chose. She took pleasure in the thought. Her life had changed so very much. Not so very long ago such things would have been impossible.

Kathy ate the remainder of her meal, feeling better for its warm sustenance as it settled in her stomach. She drained half the glass to finish, and stood to pay, counting out sufficient coins to meet the very reasonable bill.

'I hope everything was okay for you?'

Kathy nodded enthusiastically.

'It was wonderful, thank you. I haven't enjoyed a meal nearly as much in a very long time.'

'I'm glad to hear it.'

Kathy handed over the cash.

'I hope you don't mind me asking, but I'm looking for work. You don't happen to know of anything, do you?'

The waitress opened the till.

'Can you make tea and coffee?'

'Yes, yes, I can certainly do that.'

'And how about serving customers at their tables?'

'It's not something I've ever done, not professionally anyway, but I'm sure I could manage it.'

'One of my staff left to go travelling in South America a day or two back. I'll give you a two-week trial if you're interested.'

Kathy beamed.

'That would be fantastic, thank you. I'm so very glad of your offer. I nearly didn't ask at all.'

'Be here by a quarter to nine in the morning. It's minimum wage, but you'll get your meals thrown in, and we're a friendly bunch.'

Things were looking positive for Kathy, right up to the second she spotted her face emblazoned on the front of another customer's tabloid newspaper, with the large, bold headline, OFFICER ARRESTED FOR MURDER.

Kathy focussed on the floor, mumbling her words.

'I'll, um, I'll be here at eight forty-five sharp. Do I need to bring anything with me?'

'No, just bring yourself, and that will be fine. There's no need to be nervous. I'll show you how everything works before the first customers arrive. You're going to be fine.'

Kathy turned away, pulled on her coat, lowered her head and rushed out into the cold, all the time asking herself why her footfalls sounded so very loud on the wooden floor. She'd looked different in the photo, younger and with dark hair too. She'd gotten away with it, hadn't she? The reader hadn't stared. He hadn't said anything to cause alarm… But, hold on… other people would have seen the report. Hundreds, thousands, even tens of thousands conceivably. People with prying eyes. People who'd report back. Even the bastard's spies!

Kathy hurried into a quiet residential courtyard leading off the winding lane and threw up in a corner behind a large green wheelie bin as the sky darkened and the day's light began to fade. She continued wrenching, doubled over and shaking until her gut ached and there was nothing left but bile.

Kathy spat the remaining vomit from her mouth and wiped the tears from her eyes with a sleeve of her wet coat. She rose to her full height and tried to look to the positives. The newspaper report wasn't the end of her world. It wasn't a disaster. No, of *course* it wasn't. No one had said anything. She wasn't recognised. Kathy repeated it in her mind, once, then twice, before finally continuing her thought process as she walked away. There would be obstacles. There were always obstacles. No one said it was going to be easy. But she'd overcome barriers before. She had to hold her nerve, for her and for her child's sake too. A photo was just a photo and no more. Today's news was tomorrow's rubbish. She had to remain calm. What other option was there? Hold her nerve, avoid panicking whatever the provocation, and she could still beat the bastard. She could still win!

Chapter 17

Hodgson took a slurp of cooling coffee, pushed her seemingly endless piles of mainly pointless paperwork aside, and picked up the phone on the third insistent ring. 'CID, how can I help you?'

Hodgson recognised Detective Chief Superintendent Harry Watts' familiar North of England accent as soon as he opened his mouth.

'We need a chat, Sarah. Be in my office in ten minutes. I've got a couple of things to do, then I'll be ready for you. Don't be late, time is of the essence.'

'Do I need to bring anything with me, sir?'

'Anything you've got pertaining to the Conner case. It's going to be high profile. The media are all over it. We've got to be seen to get it right.'

Hodgson knocked on the head of the Criminal Investigation Department's office door, opened it reticently and peeped in.

'Are you ready for me, sir?'

DCS Watts looked up from his computer screen with his black plastic framed reading glasses perched on the very tip of his nose.

'Come on in, Sarah, take a seat. Take the weight off and try to relax. You look as if you've seen a ghost.'

She sat herself down on the opposite side of Watts' excessively large oak-veneer desk, smoothing non-existent creases from her skirt with a quick movement of her hand.

'Yes, sorry, sir, it's been a stressful few days.'

The DCS nodded his agreement.

'It's always more difficult when it's one of our own. Who'd have believed it, Michael Conner? I thought nothing could surprise me anymore, after all my years in the job. But it seems I was wrong. I actually played golf with the man. I thought we were friends.'

'He's the last person I'd have suspected.'

Watts checked his high-end Swiss sports watch, making it obvious.

'Quite so, quite so... Now, how about a quick cup of coffee before we make a start? I've got twenty minutes or so before I need to head off.'

'Um, I've not long had one.'

'The kettle's on the windowsill; there's only powdered milk, I'm afraid. My secretary's still on sick leave.'

Hodgson crossed the room.

'Remind me, Sarah, how long have you been a detective?'

She looked back at him as she waited for the water to come to the boil. 'Um, it's almost six years now. Doesn't time fly when you're enjoying yourself?'

He smiled thinly.

'I've been keeping a close eye on your career. You've done well. You're making good progress.'

Hodgson felt her face flush.

'Thank you, sir, it's good of you to say so.'

'One sugar for me. It should be there somewhere.'

She dropped a spoonful of instant coffee into each of two matching pottery mugs, adding powdered milk and finally sugar before stirring vigorously with a silver teaspoon.

'What's this about, sir?'

'You arrested Conner at the hospital, yes?'

She handed him his mug.

'Yes, yes I did.'

'And now he's in a cell awaiting interview.'

Hodgson nodded twice, asking herself where the conversation was going.

'Is there something I haven't done correctly? Is that it, or—'

'No, no, not at all,' he said, interrupting her. 'I want you to conduct the interview yourself. There's only so long we can keep him locked up without charge, the clock's ticking.'

The pitch of her voice rose an octave.

'You want *me* to do it?'

'That's what I said. Why not you?'

'I'm just a DS. I thought you'd select a more senior and experienced officer. DI Lewis is back after his holiday. Perhaps he could take the lead with me as the second interviewer. We've worked together before. It went well. We've got a good rapport.'

'Don't you think you're up to it?'

She sipped her coffee, oblivious to leaving a powdery residue on her top lip.

'No, I'm not saying that, but as you said, it's a high-profile case.'

'You're a good detective, Sarah. I'm asking you for good reason. I can make it an order if you want me to.'

Hodgson touched her throat. 'I'm just surprised you've chosen me, that's all.'

'I think there are distinct advantages in you being the lead interviewer in this particular case. Worms like Michael Conner are frightened that women will laugh at them. That they won't be taken seriously and be seen as the fatally flawed individuals they so obviously are. You're more likely to get him rattled than any male officer, however senior or skilled. Challenge Conner's ego – that's my advice. Undermine him at every turn and he may well lose control. Achieve that and he'll likely say something he later regrets. Something that trips him up. A contradiction he can't counter. We need to see the real Michael Conner. Not the usual contrived performance he presents to the world. He's clearly got issues with women. That's something we can use to our benefit. I've given this a lot of thought. We let Kathy Conner down when she needed us most. We've got to do all we can to put that right. I want the bastard nailed, and you're going to do it for me.'

'I'll give it my best shot, sir. I liked Kathy, this one's personal.'

He smiled with half his mouth. 'I've got complete faith in your ability, Sarah. You're exactly the right officer for the job. Get this right and you can look forward to promotion in the not too distant future. Go and get it done.'

Chapter 18

Conner and his young duty solicitor sat opposite Hodgson and a middle-aged career constable under her supervision and waited for the inevitable questions to begin.

'Switch on the recording equipment, constable. It's time to make a start.'

DC Smith reached to his right and flicked the switch.

Hodgson met Conner's eyes, dark sweat patches forming under both arms as she prepared to begin the interrogation. She took a slow breath through pursed lips, checked her watch, stated the time and date, and then spoke up.

'My name is Detective Sergeant Sarah Hodgson. Also present is Detective Constable Steven Smith, the interviewee Mr Michael Conner, and his solicitor Mr Malcom Jenkins. I need to remind you, Mr Conner, that you are still subject to caution. Anything you say may be used in evidence if the matter comes to court at some future date. Do you understand?'

Conner nodded once, his right eye twitching as the pressure began to build.

'Now might be a good time to remind you that I'm a senior police officer who has served this community with distinction for many years,' Conner snarled. 'I understand the rules of evidence at least as well as you do, and probably better from what I've seen of your less than impressive performance. Just get on with it, there's a good girl. And refer to me by my official rank. I'm not a civilian. Show me the respect my position deserves. The quicker we get this farce over with the better for everyone.'

'You're currently suspended from duty, *Mr* Conner. The use of your rank would not be appropriate given the circumstances.'

Conner formed his hands into tight fists below the table, picturing himself pummelling Hodgson's face to a bloody pulp as he knelt over her, pinning her to the floor.

'I'm very well aware of that, thank you, sergeant. It's an injustice, a tragic waste of my time and police resources. It's a setup, a sham. My wife has run off to goodness only knows where. She's mentally ill, confused, unreliable and untrustworthy too. It's a well-established fact, undeniable, a matter of official record. You're well aware of that, or at least you should be. I've discussed Kathy's issues with you more than once in recent weeks. You should be looking for her rather than wasting your time interviewing an innocent man.'

'Is there anything you'd like to add before we continue?'

Conner moved forwards in his seat, keen to drive home his point.

'My wife's not fit to look after herself. That's why I've had to care for her for as long as I have. I love the woman, but she's not the same person I married. It breaks my heart to even say it. If something happens to the unfortunate woman while she's out there somewhere on her own, something terrible, it's down to you.'

Hodgson picked up a thick sheaf of papers in a cardboard file, flicking through the first few pages, taking her time.

'Why did you try to kill yourself, *Mr* Conner?'

The solicitor spoke out for the first time.

'Is that relevant?'

Hodgson met his eyes.

'I'm just trying to put the allegations faced by your client in a proper context. I think that's in everyone's interests, don't you?'

Jenkins was about to further object when Conner raised a hand, stiff fingers pointed to the ceiling, his heart pounding.

'Just so everyone's crystal clear, I did *not* try to kill myself. I was drugged. I was set up. You've been conned by a crazy manipulative bitch with mental health issues. I've said all this before at the hospital. It's the only viable explanation that makes any sense at all. How many times do I have to repeat myself?'

'You tried to kill yourself, *Mr* Conner, that's a statement of certainty.'

Conner's eyes reddened as his head began to ache, pounding, booming compression and sound making him flinch.

'Are you too stupid to understand even the most basic facts? Maybe the brass should have asked someone with better detective skills to conduct the interview. A man, possibly – someone who could apply logic in a way you so obviously can't. How you became a sergeant in the first place is a complete mystery to me. What numpty made that decision? You're constable material at very best. Leave the more complex work to the grown-ups, there's a good girl.'

Hodgson shook her head slowly and deliberately, following his eyes as he looked her up and down, refusing to look away.

'You took an overdose of your wife's sleeping tablets. You took the entire bottle. That's a lot of tablets! If it weren't for the emergency services, you'd be dead and gone. You've got the paramedics and a passing witness to thank for your life. Why the continued denial? The facts speak for themselves.'

Conner placed his elbows on the table and leant towards her, as she held her position.

'No fucking way! I wouldn't do that. I didn't take the pills. I didn't take anything at all. I've never felt suicidal in my life.'

Hodgson screwed up her eyes.

'Oh, come on, Mike, there's no room for doubt. The doctors ran blood tests. The drug was in your system. That's a scientific fact, not conjecture on my part. You took the tablets. It's the only logical explanation. That's the only thing that makes any sense. It really is as simple as that. Denying it is pointless at best. Your answers are becoming ridiculous.'

Conner looked ready to explode, eyes bulging, adrenalin flooding his system as his headache intensified.

'Now, you listen to me, you sanctimonious bitch. If there were any drugs in my system, they got there without my knowledge. My wife must have given them to me. She must have slipped them in a meal or drink when my back was turned. She tried to kill me. It *was* attempted murder but on *her* part, not mine. That's the only rational explanation right there! That's what you should be focussing on. Investigate that bitch! She's a scheming, manipulative killer. Little Kathy Conner! Even I'm finding it hard to accept. I didn't think she had the guts. But that's what happened, that's the truth of it. You've got this very badly wrong. Even you should be able to see that by now. Any fool could work it out. I didn't even know she was taking sleeping tablets. I didn't know the fucking things were in the house.'

Hodgson's eyes widened, her posture stiffening, disliking him more than she ever thought possible.

'Illogical denial, smoke and mirrors, is that really the best you've got?'

Conner wiped the sweat from his brow with the back of one hand. He wanted to reach out and grab her, to punish her, to drag her across the table and pound her into submission until she accorded him the grudging respect he felt he so richly deserved.

'What the hell's that supposed to mean?'

Hodgson took a slow, deep breath, upping the pressure, in no hurry to continue.

'The empty medicine bottle was on the floor next to your bed. Your fingerprints were all over it. Your explanations are becoming more ludicrous by the second. You took the tablets yourself. You wanted to die. It's time for some honesty. This is your opportunity to explain why you did what you did. Do yourself a favour and come clean. Tell your side of the story.'

Conner pointed at her with a jabbing digit, chin high, chest puffed out, eyes flashing.

'Now you listen, and you listen well. It didn't happen the way you say, no way. I am not suicidal. I have *never* been suicidal. I keep saying it. Kathy did all this. It was her. She's not dead. She hasn't been murdered. This whole situation is ridiculous to the point of comedy. I had everything to live for. A fantastic career, the promise of promotion, a return to the plain-clothes ranks in a job I love. I'm an alpha male at the peak of his almost limitless powers. I've never felt depressed in my life.'

Hodgson tilted her head and paused, silently trying to work out if Conner were desperate, unstable, or maybe a bit of both. Yes, that was it, a bit of both.

'Why the continued pretence in the face of undeniable reality? It doesn't take an investigative genius to work it out. You know how things work. I follow the facts. They tell a story. We all know what really happened. The evidence speaks for itself.'

Conner wanted to hit out. He so wanted to hit Hodgson. To hurl her to the floor, to stamp down, to ram her questions back down her self-important throat.

'Why the *hell* are you talking about evidence? You haven't got any evidence. I haven't done anything. I'm not a criminal! I'm the victim, not the perpetrator. Get that into your thick head and you might get somewhere. Kathy drugged me and then she did a runner because she's off her fucking head. She tried to kill me and failed. Nobody has died! It's time to track her down. It's attempted murder on *her* part just like I told you. I shouldn't be here at all. She's the one who's committed a crime. Arrest her and put *her* away. Do your fucking job!'

Hodgson stifled a laugh.

'I suggest you calm yourself down before we continue. Getting worked up isn't going to do you any favours. You should understand that better than most. Or maybe you're not capable of keeping a hold on your emotions. Is that it?'

Conner gripped the table's edge with both hands, knuckles white, legs planted wide.

'Calm myself down? Are you trying to wind me up? Calming down would be a lot easier if you weren't spouting such total crap. I've been arrested on suspicion of murder, *me* – a respected police officer without a blemish on his record. It would be funny if it weren't so fucking tragic. You're not fit to be a detective. You're not even fit to be in the force. You're making a complete fool of yourself. This is going to come back to haunt you big time. It's a career-ending cock-up you're never going to recover from. I'll be back on the job before you know it. Just you wait and see.'

Hodgson drummed the table with the fingers of one hand.

'How long are you planning to keep up this pantomime? You're not convincing anyone, not anymore. People have seen through you, Mike. What did you do with the body? That's the only thing I haven't worked out yet. Are you going to help me join the dots?'

'What body? What the hell are you talking about now? There's no body to find.'

'Your wife's body! Who else did you think I was talking about? You killed her at your home. A passer-by heard her screaming before her death. It was a brutal murder. Now's the time for you to explain what happened in your own words. This is your opportunity to talk. You need to take it.'

A single bead of sweat ran down Conner's face and settled on his collar.

'She's still alive! She's hiding somewhere and laughing at us right now. I didn't kill her. I didn't kill anyone. I've said it and said it. That's my explanation, and it happens to be the truth. There's nothing more to say. Why not switch off the tape and leave it at that? I've had enough. Go and find the bitch. Leave me alone.'

Hodgson grinned sardonically.

'Oh, I *know* you killed Kathy. I know where you killed her and I know how you killed her. We're looking for her body as we speak. A search team is on the case, sniffer dogs, house to house, the lot. There's only so long a corpse can stay hidden. We'll find her. It's just a matter of time.'

He crossed and uncrossed his legs, his face reddening as he fought to retain control.

'You're not making a lot of sense, woman. You've got this horribly wrong. I haven't touched the bitch. I keep saying it. Why aren't you listening to a word I say?'

Hodgson relaxed back in her seat, gaining confidence, keen to drive home her advantage as her suspect slowly disintegrated in front of her.

'You had me fooled, Mike, you really did. I'll give you that much. I had you down as a nice guy. We all did. But it's time to drop the act. We all know what you are now. You're a liar, a bully and a killer too. It's as clear as day.'

Conner gritted his teeth and snarled.

'You're full of crap, woman. You don't know what you're talking about. You couldn't find your own arse with both hands.'

Hodgson sighed, making no effort to hide her disdain.

'Do you know? I actually felt sorry for you for a time. I swallowed all that shit you talked about your wife's mental health issues. I let Kathy down. The service let her down. Five calls for help and we gave you the benefit of the doubt. I won't be making that mistake again. What made you snap in the end? What drove you over the edge? I'd really like to know.'

Conner cracked his knuckles.

'I've got no idea what you're talking about. The only person you've let down is *me*.'

'Why kill the poor woman? I just don't understand it. If things were so bad, if your relationship was at such a low ebb, why not go your separate ways? Why not get a divorce and start a new life rather than committing murder and then trying to kill yourself? You've taken her life, ruined your career and jeopardised your freedom for years to come. Was life really that bad? Did your situation justify all that absolute horror? Or do you like hurting women? Is that it? Does it make you feel big? I can't think of any rational explanation. Perhaps you'd like to enlighten me.'

'Are you fucking stupid or something? Kathy's done a runner! She's playing you. You need to start looking for her and let me get back to work to do what I do best. Do your fucking job, woman! I'll have you back as a PC and directing traffic before you can blink.'

'Oh I don't think so, Mike. Your bullyboy days are well and truly over. The scenes of crime folk have been over every inch of your place. There's blood everywhere. It's been estimated at between four and five pints in total. There is no way in the world that any woman could lose that much blood and live. You're a murderer, and I'm going to prove it.'

Conner jerked his head back, mouth hanging open, a hand flying to his chest.

'What?'

'You heard me.'

'Four to five pints?'

'That's correct, that's what I said. Anything to say in explanation? Now would be a good time to answer.'

Conner appeared very close to panic, the sheen of perspiration on his brow threatening to become a flood.

'It can't be her blood.'

'But it is, Mike, it is. We've run DNA tests. The results were rushed through. It's Kathy's blood. One hundred per cent guaranteed with no room for doubt.'

He stared at her in utter disbelief, his mind racing, hormones speeding to his muscles, flight or fight but with nowhere to run.

'Okay, if that's true, if she's really dead as you claim, it wasn't me. I'm not guilty. Someone else must have broken into the house. Some maniac must have drugged me and then killed my wife when I was incapacitated and not in a position to protect her. The killer set me up. I've made a lot of enemies over the years. I've put a lot of people away, some for a very long time. That's the only viable explanation right there. It's the only thing that makes any sense at all. I'll repeat it on the off chance you're actually listening this time. I did *not* kill my wife. If she's dead, someone else did it. I'm an innocent man.'

'Nice try, but you were found covered in Kathy's blood with the murder weapon next to you on the floor.'

'What?'

Hodgson opened the file and pushed a ten-by-six-inch colour photo across the table.

'It was almost as if you'd bathed in the stuff. Take a look for yourself.'

Conner stared at the image, mouth agape, unable to speak as Hodgson continued.

'And your fingerprints are all over the knife's shaft, in case you were wondering. Yours and nobody else's! The evidence is indisputable. There's no room for doubt, no ambiguity, just facts that condemn. You made no effort to hide what you did, that's the reality. You didn't bother because you weren't expecting to be sitting here now. You didn't think there'd be any questions to answer, not in this world. You thought you'd be dead and gone.'

Conner shoved the photo away, unable to believe the evidence of his own eyes, not wanting to look at the image for a second longer. Not wanting to consider the implications for his future as his residual confidence drained away almost to nothing.

'But things didn't work out as you'd hoped, did they, Mike? Your implausible explanations aren't going to achieve anything at all. You sound irrational at best. It's time for the truth.'

Conner sat looking at her in trembling silence, desperately attempting to make sense of the unfathomable. Searching for words of clarification he couldn't find.

The solicitor suddenly stood, holding both hands out wide, palms faced forwards, fingers splayed.

'I'd like to take a break. I need to consult privately with my client.'

Conner reached out, clutching a sleeve of his lawyer's grey business suit and dragging him back down into his seat with a resounding thud which seemed to reverberate around the room.

'I've got nothing to say to you. I haven't broken any laws. I want to get this shit over with. Keep your fucking mouth shut, there's a good lad.' And then a line he'd used before. 'Leave the talking to the grown-ups.'

Hodgson couldn't believe her luck.

'You want to continue?'

'My God, she's actually got it. Just get on with it, woman! Let's bring this farce to a close.'

'Your bloody footprints were found throughout the house, in the bathroom, your bedroom, on the landing, on the stairs, in the hall, and in the kitchen leading directly to the back door. You butchered that poor woman in the bathroom and then you dragged her body through the house as far as the back garden. That's where the blood stops. I just don't know what you did from there. Did someone help you dispose of her body? Is that what happened? Some lowlife who owed you a favour? That's my best bet anyway. You persuaded a local criminal contact to act as a reluctant accomplice.'

'That didn't happen.'

'I suggest it did. Your accomplice took Kathy's body away for disposal while you went back upstairs to die. That's pretty close to what happened that day. Am I right?'

Conner tugged at his hair.

'You've got to listen to me, please. They weren't my footprints! I've been set up. I didn't kill her. If someone else was at the house they were the perpetrator, not some non-existent fantasy accomplice you've conjured up in your head. Whoever it was drugged me. And they killed Kathy too. They did it all.'

Hodgson rolled her eyes.

'There's no evidence to suggest that anyone else actually entered the house at any point. The footprints have all been matched to a pair of *your* shoes. *Your* shoes, Mike, not some unidentified accomplice waiting in the garden to take the body away when it suited you. There's no room for reasonable doubt. The drugs were in your system, your fingerprints and yours alone were on the murder weapon, and your bloody footprints are throughout the property. Your continued denials aren't helping you in the slightest. We've got more than enough evidence to prove that you're a killer. Solid evidence that you're finding it impossible to refute despite your best efforts. You know the score. You've been a working copper for longer than I have. You're going to be charged. You must understand that. Why not confess to your crimes and make it easier on yourself when you get to court? That's what I'd

The Girl In Red

do in your place. Look to reduce your sentence. Knock a few years off while you still can.'

Conner's shoulders slumped over his chest as he held his head in his hands. He'd never felt lower. He'd never felt so helpless or more confused. And he loathed Hodgson with every cell of his being for her part in his downfall. He wanted to hurt her. He *so* wanted to hurt her; to reach out and smash her face into the table time and again. For a second he feared he may lose control of his bowel; to actually shit himself in one adrenalin fuelled evacuation. He clenched his buttocks tightly together as he looked at Hodgson with pleading eyes filled with a combination of hate and despair.

'None of this makes any sense. Someone else did it all, someone with a grudge. Someone looking to bring me down. Look for witnesses. Knock on doors. Ask the right questions and discover the truth before it's too late. Why aren't you listening to me, woman? For fuck's sake, open your eyes and do your job. If Kathy's dead, it wasn't me!'

Chapter 19

It wasn't the first time Michael Conner had been in HM Prison Exeter, with its imposing high stone walls, located in the New North Road area of the pleasant Devonshire city. He'd been there on numerous occasions over the years, to interview one prisoner or another as part of his investigations. But this time was different, very different, and he was experiencing a creeping sense of foreboding for the first time in his adult life. He could sense danger in the air. It was eating away at him, beating him down.

Conner sat back on his prison bed and considered his situation as his gut churned like a washing machine on a spin cycle. It wasn't so much the fact that he was an alleged wife killer that placed him at risk. It was more his former professional role that had created a noticeable stir amongst the other inmates. The police were understandably unpopular amongst the incarcerated criminal classes, and he knew that he was more disliked than most.

He recognised several of his fellow prisoners in the remand unit, three of whom he'd played his part in charging and hopefully convicting once their cases reached court. To say he was loathed was perhaps an understatement, and when he walked out of his cell and stood in the entrance to the communal recreation area for the first time, he knew an attack of some kind was inevitable. He had to find the courage to stand his ground. That was key. He repeated it again and again, yelling it in his head to drown out his anxieties and silence his fears. There was no option but to front up to any potential attacker, however dangerous, however intimidating – and to be the first to strike. It was a case of survival of the fittest with no place for the weak. There were different rules in the world within the walls. The law of the jungle would inevitably prevail. He had to face that fact and act accordingly; climb to the top of the evolutionary tree, an alpha male, the king of the jungle, whatever the odds against him.

Conner took a single step forwards, then another, and another, moving steadily until he was at the approximate centre point of the large, brightly lit room. He turned in a slow tight circle, proactively portraying a relaxed and confident demeanour that belied his true feelings, chest puffed out, muscles taut, and glaring angrily at any prisoner who dared to look him in the eye. When Conner first saw the overly muscular, steroid fed man, covered in self-inflicted tattoos from head to foot, he knew an assault wouldn't be long in coming. The man was a serial offender and one he knew only too well, with his long history of severe violence and drug dealing in Devon, Cornwall and beyond. Andy Bridges was a career criminal. A seasoned offender who saw imprisonment as an unwelcome but inevitable occupational hazard – that was a price worth paying for the wealth and status his life of crime provided.

Conner looked at him and only him, as if they were the only two men in the room. The opportunity to beat up an ex-copper would be far too good to turn down. The fear of sanction was never going to be enough to hold his antagonist back. The boost to his criminal status and the satisfaction of revenge would be far too significant a payoff for that.

Conner sauntered towards the man, again portraying a degree of confidence he didn't feel, rather than slink away as his instincts dictated. He took slow, deliberate steps, his mind racing as a red mist slowly descended, an instinctive reaction driven by tension. If he was going to survive imprisonment intact, there was only one way to do it. He had to be the daddy; feared, begrudgingly respected, the cock of the walk. This was his one and only opportunity to achieve precisely that.

Conner stopped and watched the big man's every move as he rose to his feet, hands clenched and ready to strike at the first chance.

'What the fuck do you want, pig?'

Conner didn't reply. Instead, he sprang forwards, moving with surprising speed and agility, slamming a tightly clenched fist into his rival's throat, once, then twice, before standing back and watching the big man slump slowly to the floor, gasping for air, his breathing restricted like a slowly deflating blow-up toy. Conner considered stamping down on his helpless opponent's head as he writhed on the cold concrete floor, but he spotted a guard approaching in his peripheral vision and held his hands up high in the air, repeatedly claiming self-defence at the top of his voice, shouting to be heard above the resultant din as other prisoners gathered to witness the spectacle.

A young guard in his early twenties, only weeks into a job he already hated, looked down at the muscle-bound victim as he curled up in the recovery position, clutching his neck, eyes watering, a thin drool of bloody spittle running down his heavily stubbled chin. The guard shouted out in a wavering voice and pointed, ordering Conner back to his cell, before raising his two-way radio to his mouth and summoning urgent help, which to his obvious relief arrived quickly in the shape of two older and more experienced guards, who were well used to such things in their world within the walls.

The larger of the three guards strode towards Conner, stopping within six feet of him, out of striking distance, holding a hand in the air, waving him backwards as if directing traffic.

'That's it, back you go, back you go, get in your cell and close the door behind you. Now, Conner, move, man! Get on with it. You'll do exactly as you're told if you know what's good for you.'

As Conner retreated towards his cell, hands still in the air and walking backwards one considered step at a time, he beamed a face-stretching smile. Prison world had its own rules. Its own modes of acceptable behaviour. The one thing lower than a pig was a grass. That was to his advantage. His victim wouldn't be making a statement of incrimination. And neither would any of the witnesses. They'd say they'd seen nothing, heard nothing and had nothing to say. Helping the authorities wasn't the done thing in prison world. Those were the rules, never to be broken. The only version of events on official record would be his. Conner thought it through as he entered his cell and sat on his bed, rehearsing his mitigation in his mind time and again until he considered it precisely right. I was scared for my life, officer. That's all he'd have to say. I was aiming for his chin when I threw the two punches, not his throat. It was instinctive, an act of self-preservation and nothing more. I'm not a violent man by nature, far from it, in fact. The circumstances were exceptional. There was no other choice. If I hadn't hit out, it would have been me lying on that cold, hard floor. I acted within the law, with reasonable force. It was self-defence. I did the right thing.

Conner stretched out with his head on the thin pillow and closed his eyes tight shut, satisfied with his thought process. He drifted into an exhausted sleep, but within the hour he was shaken awake and marched to a solitary cell by two burly guards on the orders of the prison governor, still protesting his innocence – even claiming he shouldn't be in prison in the first place. That his incarceration was a travesty of justice. And a tragic waste of limited resources too. He was one of the good guys and not a criminal. Why couldn't the authorities see that? It was so obvious, so plain to see by anyone with even an ounce of intelligence. Conner said it and believed it. He was the victim of a miscarriage of justice. An esteemed law enforcer worthy of the guards' respect.

Conner made his impassioned case to anyone in earshot, whether they wanted to hear it or not. He hadn't killed his wife. He said it and said it. He shouted it out. He yelled it at the top of his voice, making himself heard above all others. Kathy was still alive. The bitch was still alive! The more he'd thought about it he more certain he was. The police hadn't found her body because the cow wasn't dead. She'd escaped him. Done a runner when he'd least expected it. That's why she'd dyed her hair that ridiculous shade of yellow. And the curry! She'd cooked the vindaloo to hide the taste of the medication. Of *course* she had. It seemed so very clear. He'd felt exhausted after eating it. Not just tired but poleaxed. All doubt was gone. Kathy had set him up. She was conning them all. It was far more than a suspicion; it was unfathomable truth. Conner didn't understand how she's managed it all, but she had. He didn't know the detail, not the intricate complexities of her plan, but he'd never felt more certain of anything in his life. Kathy was taunting him, mocking him despite all he'd done for her over the years. She was laughing at him in spite of his putting a comfortable roof over her ungrateful head.

Conner clasped his hands over his ears, pressing his palms against the side of his skull and holding them there. But he could still hear Kathy as clear as day. As if she was there with him. As if she were sharing his cell. He could hear her giggling now. The sound reverberating around the small room, bouncing off the walls. Kathy was cackling like the witch she was. The bitch, the total fucking bitch! How dare she? How fucking dare she?

Conner was panting hard now, his chest rising and falling in rapid rhythm as he clutched his ears still tighter. He reached out and shook a clenched fist in the air as he pictured Kathy's smirking face only inches from his. Value your freedom, bitch, take full advantage and laugh while you still can. He sank his teeth into her nose in his mind's eye, tasting her blood, appreciating its metallic tang on his tongue. His frown became a smile. One day his fantasy would become a glorious reality and not just a construct of his creative mind. He spoke it out loud and proud. Announcing it to a world that was oblivious to his dark intentions.

'You're going to suffer, you scheming mare. You worthless whore! Can you hear me, bitch? I'm coming after you. I'll never let you rest. Your time will come.'

Conner sucked the fetid air deep into his lungs to steady his pounding heart as Kathy's image slowly faded away to nothing. It was time to calm down. Time to focus. He now understood that he was likely to spend the remainder of his remand locked alone in that cell, and that, he told himself, was just fine with him. It was safer to be separated from the crowd. An undoubted bonus he hadn't adequately considered when planning his assault.

And it meant more time to think, more time to prepare with precision and necessary detail. That had to be a good thing. An added advantage. Fate was smiling on him. He was special. Better than all those who sat in judgement. Soon he'd be back in control.

Conner sat up and relaxed his shoulder muscles as the severity of his headache gradually paled. In that instant he decided to prepare for his pending court case night and day, and plan for his escape too, should the jury find him guilty despite his innocence. He'd work it all out to his best advantage. And once that was achieved, he'd rehearse the almost infinite suffering he intended to inflict on Kathy, just as soon as he had the slightest opportunity. That would be the climax. An event ultimately more satisfying than anything he'd achieved before. If the bitch thought she'd suffered, it was going to get worse. If she thought she knew the limits of pain, she was soon to learn otherwise.

He pictured Kathy prone and helpless at his feet and became instantaneously aroused. He began stroking his growing penis with one hand as he punched her to the floor in his mind's eye. He moved his hand as he imagined her shrieks becoming an ear-splitting scream that vibrated in his head, making him blink. Conner pictured himself drawing his right leg back, kicking her with all the force he could muster as he moved his hand faster, and then crushed her skull with a powerful stamp of his heel, spraying the carpet with blood and brain, as he ejaculated with a guttural groan of pleasure, endorphins flooding his system as he shot his load over his chest. Conner kept moving his hand up and down, more slowly now but still with an intense grip, until the last drop of sticky white semen seeped from the swollen tip of his erect phallus, as he pictured Kathy closing her eyes for the very last time.

He lay there, eyes wide open and focussed on the ceiling, his fantasy at a reluctant end. He wiped the ejaculate from his body with the corner of a rough grey blanket and told himself that there were good times ahead. If Kathy thought she'd won, she was very sadly mistaken. If anyone could find her, it was him. And he would, he definitely would. One way or another she'd pay the ultimate price for the inconvenience and displeasure she'd caused. Yes, she'd suffer horribly. He'd make certain of that. He'd tear her slowly apart and watch as she breathed her last strangled breath. It was no more than she deserved. Kathy was going to die at his hand. Wherever she was, wherever she was hiding. She would never escape him. It was just a matter of time. She was tried, convicted and sentenced to death by him and only him. He was judge, jury and executioner. Her demise was as inevitable as night and day. And she'd brought it on herself. He held no blame. Death was no more than the disloyal bitch deserved. Her punishment was just.

Chapter 20

Tom and Anna Oakes sat huddled in their modest lounge, staring at the television screen as an attractive dark-haired female BBC Devon newsreader presented an intense six-minute report relating to Michael Conner's arrest and remand in Exeter Prison. Anna freed herself from Tom's loving embrace as the story came to an eventual end, quickly heading for the kitchen and very much hoping that her husband of four years wouldn't ask too many unwelcome questions that she couldn't hope to answer with either the clarity or conviction that would satisfy his enquiring mind.

Anna stopped on reaching the kitchen door and spoke without looking back. 'Do you fancy a bite to eat? I'm feeling a bit peckish. There's a nice quiche in the fridge if you fancy it? Cheese and tomato with a wholemeal base. I bought it in the market at lunchtime yesterday. It would be a shame not to eat it while it's at its best.'

'Turn your head and look at me,' he said.

She looked back at him with a far from convincing smile on her lips.

'I can heat it up if you like? It wouldn't take a minute. And perhaps a chilled glass of white wine to go with it. That would complement the meal perfectly.'

Tom jumped to his feet and strode towards her, a look of genuine concern on his handsome face.

'Are you all right, Anna? Aren't you going to say something? Forget the food for goodness sake! That was Mike they were talking about, our brother-in-law. He's been charged with murdering your sister. I'm worried about you. I can't believe you're not reacting.

Just blanking it out as if it hasn't happened isn't going to help anyone at all, least of all you. What on earth's going on in your head? I want to help. Really I do. There's no need to hide your feelings. I want to know what you're really thinking. Don't hold back.'

Anna looked away.

'I've got some nice sweet onion chutney in the kitchen somewhere. What do you think? Quiche, chutney and a bit of salad?'

'Didn't you hear what I said?'

She turned to face him.

'Kathy's dead, Tom – I'm not in denial. Mike killed her, it was murder, and he deserves to be punished. That's it! I'd lock him up for the rest of his miserable life if I could. The police have to do their job. What more is there to say? If we talk about it until we're blue in the face, it's not going to make even the slightest difference. All that's left is finding the body so that we can put Kathy to rest and say goodbye properly.'

Tom placed a hand on each of his wife's slender shoulders as she opened a cupboard door, squeezing her gently as she reached for the chutney jar.

'Do you really think Mike killed her? I know Kathy sometimes claimed he was a bit of a bully, but murder... really? I find it hard to believe, to be honest. He's always seemed all right to me. I've always liked the bloke.'

'Oh, he was *much* more than a bully. He used to punch her and kick her too. He treated her like a piece of shit on his shoe. I wish she'd walked away long before it was too late.'

'Maybe she *was* mentally ill. Perhaps she made most of it up. You know... exaggerated how bad things were. She wouldn't be the first person to look for attention that way. I saw a programme about it a few months back on Channel 4. A nurse pretending to be seriously ill for years before a psychiatrist finally figured out what was going on. I think they call it Munchausen syndrome. It's far more common than most people appreciate, apparently.'

Anna felt her entire body tense.

'My sister wasn't ill. There were bruises all over her body. She miscarried after an assault. I'm not surprised he killed her. Everything she said was the truth. What happened didn't surprise me at all.'

He hesitated.

'Did you actually see Kathy's bruises? Did she ever show them to you? Or is it something she told you about, like the nurse on the telly. I'm not saying Mike wasn't a bit forceful when he lost patience, but that doesn't make him violent. And it certainly doesn't make him a killer. Maybe there's another explanation. Something we're not aware of. The police don't make everything public. They could be holding something back.'

'No, Tom, that isn't what's happening.'

He frowned as she pulled away.

'But how would you know?'

'A Sergeant Hodgson contacted me. She's asked me to call at the police station after work tomorrow. I'll be making a statement.'

'Really? What about?'

'Just what I've told you. Kathy was scared of Mike. She'd tried to leave. He was a bully. That sort of thing.'

'They'll want to know if you actually *saw* anything. And you didn't. You know what your mother thinks. She still doesn't believe a word Kathy said.'

'Do you think I don't realise that?'

Tom reached out, touching her arm.

'I'm just trying to help, Anna. I can see that you're struggling. Maybe you're not thinking straight. It wouldn't be surprising in the circumstances. It's an emotional time. You're under a great deal of pressure. I don't want you making a statement and then wishing you hadn't once it's done. Just tell the police what you know as a fact and nothing more. That's the sensible thing to do.'

'Okay, that's enough! I really don't want to hear any more. What's happened, happened. Talking's not going to change that. Mike killed my sister. I've no doubt whatsoever, and that's not going to change whatever you say. When the full facts come out you'll have to accept that and so will my mother. If anyone is in denial, it's the two of you!'

'Maybe your sister's not dead at all, they still haven't found a body. The police could have this all wrong. You have to agree it's a possibility. Maybe someone else abducted her. Or perhaps she just left herself.'

Anna took a bottle of golden Chardonnay from the wine rack, uncorked it, picked up two glasses and headed back into the lounge without repose.

Tom hurried after her.

'Kathy could still be alive, Anna, that's all I'm saying. Maybe Mike didn't kill her at all. It's too soon to give up on her. He could be an innocent man.'

Anna sat on the three-seater sofa with Tom immediately next to her, filling both glasses to the halfway point.

'You heard the news as well as I did. You heard what the reporter said. There's no room for doubt. My sister is dead. I really wish she wasn't. I wish she were still with us, but she's not. I have to accept that reality. False hope isn't going to help anyone, especially not me. You need to stop putting crazy doubts in my head. The CPS wouldn't be pursuing the case unless they were sure. They have to think there's a reasonable chance of conviction. That's how they work.'

Tom drained his glass, craning his neck to peck her cheek.

'I'm sorry, it's just all so hard to accept. It's the sort of thing that happens to other people's families. It doesn't seem real. I can't believe it's us.'

'I know, it's the same for me.'

'You sometimes seem more angry than upset. I get that, but if Kathy's dead, you've got to let yourself mourn your loss.'

'I'm going to tell the police all I know and then focus on the court case. As much for Kathy's sake as my own. She'd want Mike to pay for what he's done. And I do too. I hope he never sees the light of day again. I may be called as a prosecution witness. I've got to stay strong. I want to see him convicted and sentenced. There'll be plenty of time for tears when it's done.'

Tom moved to the very edge of the settee. 'You have told me everything, haven't you? No secrets, remember? That's the way it's always been in our relationship. There's nothing you're holding back?'

She wanted to tell him everything. She *so* wanted to tell him the truth.

'Oh, come on, Tom, why would you ask that?'

He patted her thigh.

'I'm sorry, I shouldn't have said anything. I was just sounding off, that's all. You can count on me. I love you, Anna. I'll be with you every step of the way.'

Chapter 21

Anna's entire body was trembling as she drove the short journey to the police station. It wasn't so much the idea of lying that bothered her most. It was the possibility of being caught out. Getting caught out would mean letting Kathy down, and that was unthinkable in the circumstances. Attempting to pervert the course of justice. Wasn't that what they called it? Wasn't that the legal jargon? Kathy's plan would disintegrate in an instant. And she could end up in serious trouble too. She had to stay strong, believable, persuading, and refuse to buckle, whatever the pressure.

Anna parked her French hatchback in a well-lit area of the car park close to the building's entrance, exiting and locking the car just as the sky opened and the rain began to fall. She hurried across the black tarmacadam on her two-inch heels, careful to avoid the many puddles with quick dancing feet until she reached the six concrete steps leading to impressive smoked glass double doors.

Anna entered reception to be met by an efficient female civilian member of staff in her mid to late thirties, who enquired as to her purpose and told her to take a seat in the waiting area to the side of the counter. Anna sat herself down after brief mumbled words of thanks, and only had to wait for a little over five minutes before Hodgson appeared from a nearby lift and slowly approached her. The DS raised a hand in friendly greeting.

'Mrs Oakes, Mrs Anna Oakes?'

Anna rose to her feet, trying to appear unfazed, as if she didn't have a care in the world.

'Yes, that's right. And you must be DS Hodgson.'

Hodgson nodded.

'You needn't look so nervous, Mrs Oakes. You're here as a witness, not a suspect. There's nothing to worry about. I'm grateful you've taken the time.'

'Why wouldn't I come? Kathy's my sister. I want to do anything I can to help.'

'If you follow me, I'll see which interview room's free. Do you fancy a coffee before we make a start?'

Anna followed Hodgson into a long white-painted corridor with a series of office doors to either side.

'No, not for me, thanks. I'll be heading home for tea once we're done.'

Hodgson glanced into one room, then another, and then another, before finally opening the door to interview room five.

'If you take a seat, Mrs Oakes, we'll make a start.'

She sat as instructed.

'It's Anna, please call me Anna.'

Hodgson took a statement form from a draw located directly below the small tabletop.

'Let's start with your full name, address and date of birth?'

Anna provided the information as requested, her voice quivering as she tried to hold it together.

'I'm very sorry for your loss, Mrs Oakes. I knew Kathy personally. What happened to her was a tragedy.'

Anna nodded, trying not to let her anxiety show.

'Yes, it was. It's so very hard to accept. What a way to live your life and what a way for it to end! Mike's got a lot to answer for. He made my poor sister's life a misery. I hope he rots in jail.'

'And it's my job to see that he does. That's why I've asked to see you.'

Anna shifted in her seat, unable to get comfortable.

'What do you need to know?'

'Did your sister ever tell you that Mike was violent towards her?'

'Yes, yes she did, many times over the years.'

'When was the last time?'

Anna felt her stomach churn.

'It was about three months ago.'

'We'll need to discuss every occasion before we get something down on paper, but let's focus on that last time for now. I think that's best. Did Kathy speak to you on the telephone or in person?'

'I called at the house when Mike was at work. He was on some kind of course. Kathy felt sure he wouldn't turn up unexpectedly and catch us together. It's crazy. But that's the sort of thing she had to worry about. Nothing was normal in her life.'

'And if he had come back, that would have been a problem?'

'Oh yes, that would have been a *big* problem!'

'What exactly did your sister tell you?'

Anna experienced a tingling in one arm.

'She said that Mike was becoming increasingly violent and more sadistic. He punched her to the floor and raped her. He believed he was immune from prosecution. That he could get away with anything. And for a long time he did precisely that.'

Hodgson frowned hard.

'Did Kathy suffer physical injuries as a result of the assault?'

Anna replied immediately.

'Yes, she did, bruising, severe bruising. Mike's an animal, no, he's *worse* than an animal. I hate him for what he's done.'

'Did you actually see the injuries?'

Anna clutched her hands together. Should she reply in the affirmative, yes, no, yes, no?

'Yes, yes I did. Kathy stripped off to show me her body. She had large areas of dark bruising to the right side of her ribcage and to both buttocks. And there were scratch marks on the inside of her thighs where he'd clawed at her with his nails. She was in a truly awful state. It was shocking to think Mike was capable of such a thing.'

Anna found her disdain for her brother-in-law made the lying easier.

'Kathy didn't seek medical help?'

Anna shook her head.

'She was too scared.'

'I want you to think carefully before you answer my next question… Do you think your sister was in fear for her life?'

'Oh yes, without a doubt! She told me as much. She was terrified of the man. She'd have left if she could. I really wish she had. Maybe then she'd still be alive.'

Hodgson picked up her biro.

'Okay, Mrs Oakes, thank you, that's helpful. Let's go through every incident one at a time in date order. Is that okay with you?'

'If that's what's required.'

Hodgson poised the tip of the pen above her notepad.

'I neglected to ask you what you do for a living?'

Should she lie? Should she bluff it out?

'I'm a phlebotomist.'

Hodgson's eyes widened.

'What does that involve exactly?'

'I work for the Blood Transfusion Service.'

'Doing what?'

'I er… I take blood.'

The DS pictured the Conner's blood-soaked house and feared the worst.

'You take blood!'

'Yes, that's what I said. I've been in the job for several years. What's your point?'

Hodgson bounced a foot.

'Did you sister know where you work?'

'Well, yes, of *course* she did, it's not as if it's a secret. But it's not something we ever discussed in any detail.'

'Are you sure? It seems unlikely to me.'

Anna nodded, time appearing to slow as her apprehension escalated.

'Yes, I'm certain. I couldn't be more certain. We talked about Mike's violence, we talked about the physical and psychological suffering he inflicted on her on a daily basis, and we talked about the dramatic contrast between him and the kind and gentle man

I was fortunate enough to marry. We talked about all that, but we didn't talk about my work. Not even once. Why would we? It was unimportant, of no consequence. Kathy was living with a monster. There were far more important things to discuss than my career. I always feared he may kill her one day. And now he has.'

'Is that something you'd be prepared to repeat on oath? Because you may have to. You do realise that, don't you?'

Anna swallowed hard, a tightening in her chest as the room came in and out of focus.

'It's the truth. Every single word of it. I'd be happy to swear to that in any court in the land.'

'You've no doubt?'

'I did *not* discuss my job with my sister, and I never took her blood, if that's what you're wondering. If I'm asked the question a thousand times or more, I'll say the same thing.'

Hodgson pushed her chair back and stood, meeting Anna's eyes with a darting look.

'There's something I need to do. Stay where you are. I'll be back with you in five minutes.'

The DS closed the door behind her and paced the long corridor, as Anna sat alone and wondered what was to come. Hodgson walked one way and then the other, striding back to almost the exact point she began. The Blood Transfusion Service! It was one hell of a coincidence. Maybe too much of a coincidence. An element of reasonable doubt, that's all the defence would need to secure a not guilty verdict. What if Conner had been set up? What if Kathy had gone to extraordinary lengths to escape his deadly clutches with her sister's help? It wouldn't be difficult for a competent barrister to plant that doubt in a jury's minds. Conner could potentially escape justice despite the almost overwhelming weight of evidence. After all he'd done, he'd be free to victimise some other poor woman, making her life a misery. And where was the justice in that?

Hodgson allowed the wall to support her weight as she pondered her dilemma. Michael Conner was a vicious bully who'd killed his wife. A problematic and manipulative man who'd do anything and everything he could to avoid paying for his crimes. Hodgson felt sure of it. He'd committed the murder and deserved to serve his time.

She opened the door and returned to her seat, as Anna stared across at her in uneasy silence.

'It's time to write the statement, Mrs Oakes. We're going to go through each and every time your sister told you about her husband's violence, and crucially every time you saw injuries. We can take our time and record each incident in logical, sequential order from the first occasion to the last. You need to give me as much detail as you possibly can and identify specific dates and times whenever possible. And just so we're clear, I'm in total agreement that your career choice is of no relevance to the case. I won't be recording the nature of your employment on paper. We don't need to discuss your job again. Are we in agreement?'

Anna nodded twice.

'Yes, I understand. I can remember everything that happened. It's imprinted on my mind never to be forgotten. I'll describe every bruise, every scratch, every cut. Let's get it done.'

Chapter 22

Kathy was beginning to settle into her new life as she leaned against the wooden counter at the stylish cafe. She almost hadn't gone back at all after the newspaper incident. It had shaken her. So much depended on her anonymity. But now she was glad she'd returned. The cafe offered opportunity, for her and her unborn child. And she was determined to make it work, whatever the risks, whatever the dangers. The staff and the majority of customers were pleasant enough company, and no one had recognised her despite the alarming media attention, that thankfully was gradually dissipating with each day that passed. That was the best thing of all. Her continued secrecy surprised and pleased her. It felt almost as if she were an ordinary person. As if she'd never met her husband. As if he'd never existed. As if he hadn't ruined her life for so very long, like an invasive disease eating away at her well-being and self-worth. Things, Kathy told herself insistently, were going her way at last. She was still walking a metaphorical tightrope with danger on every side. There was no escaping that reality, however much she wanted to. Her fear still sometimes tread down on her chest as heavily as her husband ever had, even in his worst excesses. But there was a potential victory on the distant horizon. The sun was rising in her dark and foreboding world of woe. She could see the light and could almost touch it too. She clung on to hope like a determined limpet. She wouldn't let her fear win.

Kathy's newly acquired cheap-as-chips, pay-as-you-go mobile phone rang and made her jump at just gone twelve that afternoon, as she served two women in their seventies with freshly made vegetable cawl and crusty wholemeal bread baked locally. Kathy smiled nervously, turned away and held the phone to her face without speaking.

'Hello, Hazel, it's John… the social worker. Sally gave me your number. She swore me to secrecy. I won't be giving it to anyone else without asking you first.'

Kathy's posture slumped, a slow smile forming on her face.

'Oh, hello, John, I'm at work. Give me a second.'

She approached her friendly red-haired boss, who was making camomile tea behind the cluttered serving counter.

'Is it okay if I take my break, Mandy? The social worker I told you about is on the phone. It won't take long, promise.'

Mandy poured boiling water into two porcelain cups before looking up and smiling.

'No problem, ten minutes, yeah? It's going to get busier as lunchtime approaches.'

'Thanks, it's appreciated.'

Kathy sat in a quiet corner next to a lukewarm radiator, pressing the phone to her ear.

'Hi, John, I'm back.'

'So tell me, where are you working?'

'At the vegetarian cafe in Merlin's Lane. Do you know it?'

'Yeah, I do, I've called in once or twice, nice place. You don't hang about. I guess you're not going to need that benefit we talked about after all.'

Kathy's expression softened.

'I'm still a nervous wreck most of the time, but things are working out better than I could have hoped. I've fallen on my feet with this place.'

'That's really good to hear. How are you finding the hostel? Are you settling in?'

'Um, yeah, I like it, they're a good bunch, but I'm going to be moving.'

'What, as quickly as that?'

'One of the other girls working here lives in a small alternative community in the countryside a few miles outside town. They grow a lot of their own food and support each other in any way they can. The communal idea appeals to me. I like the sound of it. I can help with the younger children and do a bit of cooking when needed. There's a caravan available at very low rent I should be able to afford if I'm super careful with my spending. It seems like too good an opportunity to miss.'

'That all sounds great, Hazel – how soon are you making the move?'

'It's all happening the day after tomorrow.'

'Ah, okay, as soon as that. Does Sally know?'

Kathy quickly turned away as a man she hadn't seen before sat at a nearby table, glancing in her direction.

'Yes, yes, I told her as soon as I knew.'

'I'm surprised she didn't tell me.'

'Maybe she was waiting for me to do it myself.'

'Yes, that makes sense. I'm pleased for you, Hazel. Things finally seem to be going your way after all you've been through.'

Kathy raised an eyebrow.

'Does this mean you're going to be my social worker?'

'Yes, it does, I was allocated your case earlier today. I pulled a few strings. I hope that's okay?'

She smiled.

'Thank you, I'm pleased that you did.'

'I'd like us to get together at least once before Christmas. How would you feel about me visiting you at your new home at the end of the week?'

'Um, yeah, I can't see why not.'

'Have you got the address?'

She took a single sheet of paper from a trouser pocket, unfolded it, and read out a series of directions in a hushed voice, wanting only him to hear.

'So, it's right then left, then right again opposite the farm?'

Kathy checked her notes.

'Yes, and then one final left up the small track with the wooden gate. You'll see the caravan amongst a clump of trees.'

'Sounds beautiful!'

'It's peaceful, that's the main thing. London seems a very long way away.'

'What time do you finish work on Thursday?'

Kathy raised a hand to her heart. 'Just after five.'

'I could meet you at the cafe and give you a lift home if that works for you? It's not out of my way, and it would give us time to talk.'

'Um, yeah, that would be great. As long as it's not too much trouble.'

'It's no trouble at all... have you thought any more about talking to the police?'

Kathy stopped breathing for a moment and hoped he didn't hear it.

'No, it's out of the question, no police! I thought I'd made that perfectly clear.'

Her boss leant over the counter, pushing the kettle aside.

'Are you okay, Hazel?'

Kathy nodded, forcing an improbable smile before returning her attention to her call.

'Are you still there, Hazel?'

'Yes, I'm still here.'

'Look, I'm going to have to liaise with the local police child protection team sometime in the near future. But you needn't worry about it. Your husband is in London and you're here, three hundred miles away. There's no immediate risk. And no one can *force* you to give any details you don't want to give, as I said before. Just keep that in mind.'

'Do you *really* have to speak to them? Couldn't I just talk to you?'

The social worker remained silent for a full second.

'Yes, sorry, I do. But, trust me, that's okay. They're there to help you. The same as I am. This is the sort of stuff they deal with on a daily basis.'

Kathy blew out a series of sharp breaths as she rose to her feet. 'Then, I guess that's something else I'm going to have to deal with.'

'Everything's going to be absolutely fine, Hazel. There's a support network in place to help you. We won't let you down. Just you wait and see.'

Kathy was beginning to wish she hadn't visited the social services office at all. 'I'll see you on Thursday.'

'I'll look forward to it.'

She smiled. Oh yeah, you'll count the minutes. 'Thanks for ringing.'

'Bye for now, I'll let you get back to work.'

Chapter 23

'There's a Mr Vince May in reception, sarge. He asked to speak to whoever's heading up the Conner investigation. I guess that's you.'

Hodgson sighed.

'I was just about to grab a sandwich.'

Dawson glanced at his watch.

'I can see him for you, if you like? I've got half an hour or so before I need to head out again.'

'No, you're all right, ta. It's something I'd better do myself. You never know, he may have something useful to tell us. We could do with a break.'

'If you're sure?'

'How's the house-to-house going? Anything I don't know about?'

Dawson shook his head.

'No, nothing, it seems no one saw a damned thing. Or at least not that they're telling me about. And it wouldn't be hard to avoid any cameras if you know the area. Keep away from the main streets, stick to the back roads, simple as.'

'Someone transported Kathy's body from that house. It's the one hole in our case. There has to be a witness somewhere. We've just got to find them.'

'Maybe he's downstairs waiting for you now.'

The DS crossed the fingers of her right hand.

'Let's hope so, Chris, let's hope so. A murder conviction may prove difficult to achieve in the absence of a body, even with the strength of evidence. That's what I'd be focussing on if I were the defence barrister.'

'You're not having any doubts are you, sarge?'

Her expression hardened.

'The bastard killed her, Chris. We've just got to prove it.'

Hodgson entered reception to be met by a smartly dressed, well-tanned man in his mid to late fifties, who had a face-stretching smile on his ruggedly handsome face. He stood quickly as the DS approached him, reaching out a manicured hand and shaking hers, not too firmly but not too limply either.

'Mr May, Mr Vince May?'

May nodded.

'Guilty as charged.'

She ignored his effort to lighten the mood.

'My name is Detective Sergeant Sarah Hodgson. You asked to speak to an officer involved in the Conner case.'

'Yes, that's right. I may have some relevant information to share. I'm keen to help if I can. I hope I'm not wasting your time.'

Hodgson thought he appeared nervous despite the outwardly confident persona he was presenting.

'Let's find a free room, and you can tell me what you know. Let me be the judge of what's relevant. I find that's best.'

Hodgson led the man to a small interview room, pointing to a free chair on the near side of a square table.

As he sat, Hodgson retrieved a statement form from a grey metal filing cabinet at the back of the room.

'If we could start with your full name, address, date of birth and contact details, please, Mr May, that would be useful.'

He cleared his throat before providing the information as required.

Hodgson's eyes widened.

'You live in the same street as the Conners?'

'Yes, our place is almost directly opposite theirs. We were living there long before the Conners moved in.'

'Did you know them personally?'

'No, I wouldn't go as far as to say that. We never saw much of Mrs Conner, but I've exchanged pleasantries with the husband a few times over the years. "Good morning", "shame about the weather", "nice day for it"... you know, that sort of thing. The usual mundane niceties we Brits exchange with acquaintances to avoid actually talking about anything meaningful.'

'You said *we* never saw much of Mrs Conner?'

'I was referring to my wife and myself. The kids are all grown up. There's just the two of us these days.'

Hodgson leant forwards in her seat, keen to continue, rushing her words.

'So, what have you got to tell me?'

He made an unnecessary adjustment to his necktie, loosening it slightly before retightening the knot.

'Um, I er, I saw someone leaving the Conner's house through the side gate about an hour or so before the police arrived on the evening Mrs Conner disappeared.'

Hodgson's eyes appeared cold, hard, flinty, as she sat bolt upright.

'You do realise this is a murder case, don't you?'

'Yes, I do.'

'Then why the hell did you leave it so long before coming in to talk to us? You must have realised your information could be important to the investigation. Every second matters. You should have contacted us long before now.'

May's face reddened.

'We were flying to Tenerife from Bristol Airport later that night to celebrate our twenty-fifth wedding anniversary. We left the house shortly after I saw the police car screeching to a halt outside the house. I only found out about the murder when we arrived back in the UK earlier today. It was something of a shock, to say the least. I came to see you as soon as I got my thoughts together. I don't think that's unreasonable, do you?'

Hodgson responded in a soft, halting, conciliatory voice, her head tipping to one side.

'Okay, I understand, enough said. I appreciate any assistance you can offer. Think back to that evening. You saw who exactly?'

'I saw a woman, a woman with platinum-blonde hair and wearing glasses. Someone I hadn't seen before. I'm sure she doesn't live in the street. It's a relatively close community. Everyone knows everyone else.'

'Try to focus please, Mr May. Are you certain you didn't recognise her?'

He shook his head.

'No, I'd not seen her before or since.'

Should she ask? Yes, the defence would. That was inevitable. There was no avoiding it.

'This may seem like a peculiar question given the nature of the case, but could the woman you saw have been Mrs Conner?'

His forehead wrinkled.

'Are you saying she may still be alive?'

'Just answer the question, Mr May.'

'The woman I saw *wasn't* Mrs Conner. I can say that with absolute certainty.'

'You seem very sure for someone who says he's seen very little of Mrs Conner. Would you like to explain?'

'I'm an amateur artist, a portrait painter with an appreciation of the female form. I have an excellent memory for faces, the shape of a nose, the line of the lips, the length of a slender neck. The little details tend to stick in my mind.'

Hodgson noted his response in black ink. 'Okay, let's move on. Where were you when you saw the woman leave the Conner's property?'

'Um, I was in our bedroom at the front of the house. I looked out to see what the weather was doing just as she came through the gate from the back garden. I remember thinking that she looked a little anxious. She was glancing to each corner of the street with rapid movements of her head. As if on full alert.'

'You were in your house on the other side of the street. It was dark, cloudy. How clearly could you possibly have seen her?'

He appeared agitated by Hodgson's observation, his hands moving in jerks.

'I've got excellent eyesight. Better than driving standard even without glasses. And the woman walked directly under a street lamp. I considered it in great detail on my way here. Take my word for it. I saw her well enough.'

Hodgson rubbed her chin.

'Okay, I want you to think back to that night. Is there *any* possibility that the woman you saw came out of the *neighbouring* house rather than the Conner's property? Think hard, please. Your reply could be crucial to the investigation.'

'The woman came through the Conner's gate. That's the way it was. That's what I saw. I'm certain of it.'

'And you're sure you saw her leaving the Conner's back garden on that precise day, the sixth of December? Could it have been a different day? The day before or the day after possibly? If you've got even the *slightest* doubt, now's the time to say so. No one's going to hold it against you if you change your mind. It's better to say it now rather than in the witness box should you be called to give evidence at some future date.'

'Do you think I may be called as a witness?'

'It's a strong possibility given what you're telling me.'

He nodded reticently, resigned to the legal process.

'Are you beginning to have doubts, Mr May? Things aren't always as clear as they first seem. We haven't committed a statement to paper as yet. Make sure you get your story straight before you do. Take as long as you need.'

May raised an eyebrow.

'As I've already explained, we were travelling to the airport that evening. The woman I saw left the Conner's property on the sixth of December, approximately an hour before I heard a wailing siren and saw a police car pulling up outside the house. An ambulance arrived shortly afterwards. It wasn't the day before and it wasn't the day after. It was the sixth of December just as I said. Word in the street is that the Conner's had a great many arguments. Mrs Conner had serious mental health issues. I don't know if you're aware of that? Mr Conner made no effort to hide the fact. It's common knowledge with neighbours.'

Hodgson unfolded the statement form, placing it on the tabletop in front of her.

'Thank you, Mr May, that's all very concise. Now, I'd like you to give me as full a description as possible of the woman you saw that evening, and then we'll move on to get your statement down on paper.'

'I get the distinct impression that you're not entirely satisfied with my evidence. I hope I haven't wasted your time. That's the last thing I'd want.'

The DS was wishing he hadn't come at all.

'Not at all, we're always grateful for the public's help. Tell me everything you can regarding the woman's appearance, approximate age, height, build, mode of dress, hair style and length, demeanour, everything you can remember. Please be as detailed as you possibly can and tell me if you're unsure. It's important not to guess. If you're not sure, just say so.'

He provided the information as requested, beginning to enjoy the process, and then added, 'And now that I think about it, she was carrying a bag in her right hand.'

'A bag?'

'Yes, an orange carrier bag. As if she'd been doing some shopping.'

'There was something in it?'

'Oh yes, it looked fairly full, as I recall. Do you think she'd stolen something from the house? That may explain it.'

'You mentioned that you thought that the woman's glasses looked strangely out of place. Can you expand on that for me?'

'I don't think I actually used the word *strangely*, but yes, they looked more suited to sunny climes than the English winter. I think that's a fair way of putting it.'

'Sunglasses?'

'No, not exactly sunglasses, but slightly tinted, large and seemingly too big for her face. As if she'd either made a bad choice of style or borrowed them from somebody else.'

Hodgson jittered a foot against the floor.

'You thought that odd at the time?'

'Um, well, perhaps not so much at the time, but when I think about it now. A great deal has happened since to focus the mind. One doesn't expect to return from holiday to discover that a neighbour has been murdered while you were away.'

Hodgson's eyes tightened. A harried expression dominating her features.

'I appreciate that you've been very clear in what you've said up to now, Mr May, but I'm going to ask you one final time. Is there even the *slightest* possibility that the woman you saw that night was Kathy Conner, if her hair were dyed or if she were wearing a wig and glasses with which you weren't familiar?'

His reply was immediate, no hesitation, no delay.

'I can see where you're coming from with this but no, I really don't think so.'

'You said, *think so*. That suggests a degree of doubt on your part. Am I correct?'

He sighed loudly, no longer making any effort to hide his exasperation

'You're playing with words, sergeant. I've told you what I saw in clear unambiguous terms. I can't do any more than that. The woman I saw that night was a stranger to me. She wasn't Mrs Conner, and she's never going to be Mrs Conner however many times you ask me. I've got nothing more to add. There's absolutely no doubt in my mind.'

Chapter 24

There was an edge to DCS Watts' voice. A tension Hodgson had heard before, but only in times of crisis.

'Follow me, sergeant, we can talk as we walk. I need to update you on a few developments in the case.'

Hodgson hurried alongside him as he crossed the busy police HQ car park, waiting for him to share whatever bad news she knew was undoubtedly coming her way.

'Still no joy finding the corpse?'

'I'm afraid not, sir. House-to-house enquiries have come up with nothing, and whoever transported the body from the house wasn't caught on camera at any stage of their journey. I thought the press release may result in someone coming forward with relevant information at some point, but it didn't happen the way I wanted it to. We've just had the usual nutters confessing to crimes they couldn't possibly have committed. Most of them historical. If someone knows where Kathy Conner is, they're not telling me about it.'

Watts increased his pace as the sky darkened and large drops of rain seemingly came from every direction at once, bouncing off the tarmac.

'There's something I need to share with you, Sarah. It's not good news, I'm afraid.'

She screwed up her face.

'If someone else is taking over the case, I can't say I'm surprised. I thought you'd have reallocated it to a more experienced officer long before now.'

He unlocked the driver's door of his estate car with the click of a button and got in with the door left ajar, leaving her standing in the rain.

'I've had the CPS on the phone.'

She crossed and uncrossed her arms, fearing the worst.

'What did they have to say for themselves?'

'There's no easy way of telling you this. They're dropping the case. It's official. I only found out myself yesterday morning. It's going to be all over the media soon enough. I wanted you to hear it from me first. You did your best to secure a conviction in difficult circumstances. But it wasn't enough.'

Hodgson held her hands out wide, oblivious to the worsening weather as the rain turned to sleet.

'What? It's not even going to trial? That's ludicrous! Let a jury decide. That's all I'm saying. There's more than enough evidence to put Conner away. Even without a body. It's got to be worth a try, hasn't it? What have we got to lose?'

'The matter's closed, Sarah; the decision's made. I'm not any happier about it than you are, but that's the reality. It's out of my hands. We've got to accept the situation and move on.'

She took a quick step forward as he attempted to close the door.

'Oh, come on, boss. Talk to whoever's in charge. Twist their arm. Make them change their mind.'

The DCS switched off the engine, glaring up at her.

'Do you think I haven't tried?'

'What about the evidence, the tablets, the blood, the knife?'

He tapped his finger on the steering wheel.

'Someone else was at the house at the relevant time. Someone you haven't been able to identify despite all the resources we've thrown at it. That changes things. You know that as well as I do. Conner's a well-respected officer with multiple commendations on his record. We needed a watertight case. The CPS no longer think there's a realistic chance of a conviction.'

'That's totally crazy!'

'It's their decision, not ours. That's how the system works. There's nothing more I can do.'

She wiped the freezing water from her face as he restarted the engine. 'Conner's fingerprints were all over the knife. And the footprints, what about the footprints? They belonged to him, not some woman we haven't identified yet. He was plastered in blood from head to foot.'

'The decision is made, Sarah. It's too late unless we can come up with new evidence. What part of that don't you understand?'

'I just can't believe what you're telling me. The bastard's going to get away with it after all he's done!'

Watts looked away.

'There's something else.'

And just when she'd thought things couldn't get any worse.

'What is it?'

'DI Conner will be returning to work.'

Hodgson's eyes widened, the whites flashing.

'He's what? Surely you're not letting that slimeball work as a police officer again after everything he did to that unfortunate woman? Where's the justice in that? It's a travesty. Come on, boss. You need to think again.'

Watts switched on the car's wipers, adjusting the speed.

'He'll be back at his desk this coming Monday. Get used to it, Sarah. In the eyes of the law, he's an innocent man.'

Hodgson stood staring at the car as her boss reversed out of his personal parking space and drove towards the open road. She wanted to scream. She wanted to stamp and shout like a petulant toddler. But instead, she turned and hurried back towards the nearby building, as the icy rain soaked into her clothes right down to her cotton underwear. Sometimes police work was hard to bear. Sometimes the stresses made her weep. There was no shame in that. And now was one of those times.

Chapter 25

Kathy sat in her small static caravan and counted her blessings as the day slowly turned to night. The place was far from luxurious, but it was peaceful, it was remote, it was off the grid – and the other residents of the ramshackle community had made her even more welcome than she could have hoped. They were a good bunch if a little eccentric, with their own stories to tell; so unlike the man she'd married.

Kathy removed her blue jeans, lay back on her single bed, and began to read, escaping into a fantasy world of fairies, goblins and wizards at the behest of an author whose words moved backwards and forwards in time, engendering a range of emotions with seemingly effortless ease. She read a few more pages in the light of a single forty-watt bulb, stopped to make a cup of warming peppermint tea, then read some more until she felt the need for sleep an hour or so later. Kathy placed her empty cup to one side, made a quick toilet visit, and then tucked herself under a chequered Welsh wool blanket, bought cheaply in a Caerystwyth charity shop recommended by the social worker she now considered an unlikely friend as well as a source of professional help.

Kathy pulled the blanket even more tightly around herself, feeling warm, safe and secure right up to the second she closed her eyes for the first time that night. But then there he was... in her mind's eye; hovering over her like a malicious and spiteful ghost she couldn't hope to escape. Just like before. Just like always. The thoughts were repetitive. A dark mantra that was all too familiar.

Kathy placed the palms of both hands on her swollen abdomen and tried to think nice thoughts, to drive Conner's savage face from her mind. To send him to oblivion, never to return. But his image reappeared every time she sought to sleep. He haunted the darkness. There he was again. That devil in human form she knew so very well. Would she ever forget him? Would he ever become an unremembered memory? It may happen one day. It could, couldn't it, with time? Of *course* it could, of *course* it could. Kathy repeated it in her mind, yelling it time and again, attempting to drive out her doubts. It could happen one fine day but it hadn't happened yet.

Kathy lifted herself into a seated position, her eyes wide open – but her melancholy mood wouldn't lift. Her internal life was intense, with vivid colours, smells and sounds. She thought she heard his voice on the wind, as it blew through the surrounding trees. Conner was taunting her, threatening her, as he whispered in her ear. Perhaps a little music would help her. It would, wouldn't it? Maybe put on the radio to keep her company for as long as required. That would drown out his voice. That would shut the bastard up.

Kathy lay back down, a little out of breath, and listened, singing along to one three-minute song after another as her tension slowly faded. She paid only passing interest as the news began. But a short report near to the end of the programme made her jump up and take note, as she listened intently to every single word. A Plymouth police inspector had been released from prison after his murder charge was dropped. A police officer named Michael Conner. The investigation was ongoing, but the officer would return to regular duties.

No, no, no! This isn't happening. It really can't be happening! Kathy threw open the caravan door and hurled the radio out onto the stone-strewn, semi-frozen ground with all the strength and force she could muster. The bastard, the absolute bastard! He was free, free to come after her. Free to hunt them down.

Kathy clutched at her hair in clumps with both hands as her tears began to flow. How could it happen? How on earth could it happen? He'd always claimed he could get away with anything. He'd always said she'd never escape him, whatever she did – however hard she tried. And now he was out of prison, her plan in tatters. It had said so on the radio, in plain language, undeniable, unequivocal, as clear as day.

Kathy slumped to the caravan's floor as concerned residents approached from nearby dwellings. It seemed her husband was some sort of superhuman. An evil creature impervious to harm. That was the only logical conclusion. The one thing that made any sense at all. Oh God, please God, no. He'd be coming after her. And the baby too. It seemed every threat the bastard made was true.

Chapter 26

'Aren't you going to welcome me back with open arms, Sarah? Why the scowl on that pretty face? Don't hold back. We're the only people here. Now it's your chance to show me how much you've missed me.'

Hodgson recoiled in her seat.

'Have you no shame? I can't believe you've had the nerve to come back at all.'

Conner placed both hands on her desk, standing over her, holding her reluctant gaze.

'I think you'll find it's "I can't believe you've had the nerve to come back here at all, sir". Don't forget the sir. You're still a sergeant, and I'm still an inspector. And I'm going to use my superior rank to make every minute of your working life as miserable as feasibly possible for as long as I can. I may even ask to be allocated my wife's case. I couldn't do a worse job of it than you did, you fucking halfwit. It's so good to be back in the fold.'

Hodgson pushed back her chair, her skin crawling as he stood between her and the door.

'You think you're so very clever, don't you, Mike. You think everyone's convinced by your fantasy version of events. But they're not. I'm not for one. It's only a matter of time before new evidence emerges. Kathy's body will be found. And then you're going to pay for what you did to that poor woman. I'll make it my personal mission in life to see that you do.'

Conner reached across her desk, pulled her towards him and pecked her on the cheek, poking out his tongue and licking her ear as she tensed.

'Has anyone ever told you that you're lovely when you're angry, Miss Hodgson? It's quite a turn on. You may have noticed the swelling in my trousers.'

Hodgson dragged herself free, slapping him hard across his face with an open hand.

'Get out of my room, you piece of shit. Go on, now! Get the fuck out!'

He chuckled to himself as he slowly approached the door.

'Kathy is still alive. And I'm going to find her. And when I do, it's her who'll suffer. I'll expect an apology on bended knee when you finally accept the truth, and maybe a blowjob or two.' He made a sucking sound through pursed lips. 'Gobble, gobble, what do you think? Are you up for it? Your mouth's big enough even for me.'

Hodgson narrowed her stance, a bitter taste in her mouth as she glared in his direction. 'What did Kathy ever do to deserve a filthy scumbag like you?'

He turned on reaching the doorway, winking once before blowing her a kiss.

'I know you're just playing hard to get, Sarah. I know what you women are like. Gagging for it, wet and waiting, whenever you're paid a little attention by any man in the vicinity.'

Hodgson's eyes flashed white, spittle forming at the corners of her mouth. 'Get out! Get the fuck out!'

Conner clutched his engorged genitals through his trousers, thrusting his hips forwards.

'If you want me, all you have to do is say so.' And then a line he'd used before; one of his favourites – a line of which he was proud. 'I'm man enough for any woman, and more than enough for you.'

Chapter 27

Conner parked fifty meters or so from the Oakes' terraced home, and watched from his patrol car as Tom left the house, carrying his golf clubs, about ten minutes later. Conner waited with increasing impatience until Tom drove away, and then approached the front door in full dress uniform, silver buttons polished and gleaming in the unseasonal winter sunshine. He knocked with gradually increasing force, standing back and glancing from window to window; up, down; right to left and back again when he didn't receive a reply.

Conner stood on the uneven pavement and stared at a first-floor window with a deep frown forming on his face. The curtain had moved. The bitch was peeping out. She was definitely in.

He returned to the wooden door with its shiny chrome furniture and began hammering it with the side of one fist, all the time imagining Anna Oakes cowering in her bedroom hiding place and praying he'd disappear. Conner began pounding the door with even greater force as it shuddered in its frame. He started shouting now, yelling, in danger of losing control as his rage intensified.

'Come on, Anna, open the fucking door, woman! I know you're in. There's a light on. I can hear the radio playing. You moved the curtain. Open the fucking thing. I can kick it in if you want me to.'

Conner stopped and listened, peaking through the letter box as Anna slowly descended the stairs towards the hall. And then the door opened with the chain on, Anna Oakes peeping through the gap.

'What do you want?'

He took off his cap, placed his face close to the six-inch gap and grinned.

'Naughty, naughty, aren't you going to invite me in? It's not polite to leave an esteemed visitor standing on the doorstep in the cold.'

Anna gripped the edge of the door as her legs threatened to buckle.

'Just say what you came to say and go.'

'Now, you listen to me, and you listen well. I'm going to give you two choices. You can ask me in to discuss recent events in a rational manner, or I can put my shoulder to the door, arrest you, drag you to the station in cuffs and charge you with perverting the course of justice. If you think that pathetic chain's going to stop me, you're kidding yourself. Make your choice.' He pushed up his sleeve and looked at his watch. 'You've got ten seconds from now.'

Anna unfastened the chain with fumbling fingers.

'I don't know what you think you're going to gain by this.'

'Just open the door, woman. You're almost as useless as your sister.'

Anna turned away, trembling as he followed her down the hall towards the lounge. She stood and waited while he sat in a convenient armchair with his legs spread wide.

'I asked you what you want?'

'Take a seat, Anna, there are things we need to discuss.'

She chose a chair at the furthest point from his, suddenly claustrophobic, the walls closing in.

'I've got nothing to say to you.'

Conner moved his seat towards her, hands clenched.

'Where is she?'

'I don't know why you think I know the answer to that.'

'Where is she, Anna? We can do this the easy way or the hard way. Make your choice. It's up to you.'

'I haven't seen Kathy since before your arrest. There's nothing I could tell you, even if I wanted to.'

His eyes flashed.

'So, you're admitting she's alive.'

'I didn't say that.'

Conner sniggered.

'Oh, come on, Anna, you can do better than that. I know the bitch is alive. And I know you helped her escape. If not you, then who? She must have told you where she's going. And I'm willing to bet she's been in touch since getting there. You two are close. You're like two rotten peas in a pod. Tell me where she is, and I'll leave you alone to get on with your life. Continue to protect her, and I'll destroy you. I can't be any fairer than that.'

Anna's pallid features turned ashen, a visible pulse on her neck throbbed.

'You're the worst thing that ever happened to Kathy. I wish she'd never met you. I'm not telling you a damned thing.'

Conner began slowly pacing the room, first one way and then the other.

'Wouldn't it be a shame if Tom was arrested. Wouldn't it be awful if child porn was discovered on his computer, or class A drugs found in his car? Or maybe both, what about both? That would result in a certain prison sentence. And nonces don't do well in custody. They don't do well at all. He'd be hated, targeted, treated like shit. Tom's not a hard man. He'd be eaten alive.'

Anna began to cry.

'You wouldn't d-do that. Tom's a good m-man. You know that. What has he ever done to you?'

'Where is she, Anna? That's all you've got to tell me. Give me the answer I'm looking for, and I'll leave you in peace. What have you got to lose? It seems like a good deal to me.'

'No! You can make however many threats you like. I'll tell Tom all about it. And I'll talk to your superiors too. I'll report you. I'll make it official. I'm not t-telling you a thing.'

Conner reached out, stroking her face, licking the tears from his fingers.

'Oh dear, how very sad! That would be by far the worst decision you ever make. The consequences would be dire, for you and for that ineffectual husband of yours. If you think Kathy suffered, it's nothing compared to the torrent of pain I'd inflict on you.'

Anna was weeping now, the tears running down her face as she pressed herself against the backrest of her chair.

'Just go! Please, go and leave us a-alone.'

Conner stood with his knees touching hers, calmer now, as he spoke in monotone, his voice unchanging in pitch and all the more chilling.

'I want you to go to the kitchen, I want you to make me a cup of coffee, and I want you to think very carefully while you're doing it. Maybe then you'll see sense. Why make me destroy your lives when I'm going to find Kathy anyway? Why not make it easier on yourself, and on Tom too? Anything that happens to him will be *your* fault. Think about *that* while waiting for the kettle to come to the boil. This is your final opportunity to avoid disaster.'

Anna rose to her feet, elbows pressed to her sides as she approached the kitchen door.

Conner waited for her to leave the room before delving into a tunic pocket and placing a tiny wireless listening device, linked directly to his smartphone, underneath the leather sofa, just an inch from the wall. He then put a second identical device to the right side of a large Victorian family Bible on a high shelf at the opposite side of the room, before returning to his seat.

'Is that coffee ready? I haven't got all day.'

Anna grabbed her mobile from a work surface, intending to contact Tom, but her heart sank on realising it needed charging.

She called out, 'I'll be with you in a couple of minutes, it's nearly done.'

'And not before time. What is it with you and your sister? You're both next to fucking useless.'

Anna appeared in the doorway with a mug in each hand.

'Is there really a need to swear?'

Conner laughed on accepting his drink.

'I would have thought that's the least of your worries. Have you considered your situation? You've had more than enough time to think. Are you going to tell me where the bitch is or are you going to suffer the consequences?'

'Would it make any difference if I beg?'

'Well, it would be amusing in a pathetic sort of way, but no, it wouldn't make any difference at all.'

'You're a bully, Mike. It's the only word for you. Even my mother will have to accept that after this. Are you incapable of even the most basic humanity?'

'What's your decision? You're walking a tightrope. It's the most important choice of your life.'

Anna glared at him with burning eyes, her angst turning to indignant rage.

'I've already told you that I've got no idea where my sister is. And I wouldn't tell you even if I did. You can do your worst. Now get up and get out of my house before I start screaming. These walls are paper thin. I'll say you assaulted me. I'll tell everybody you touched me sexually. You're not the only one capable of making false allegations. I could be surprisingly convincing if needed. Sooner or later, mud's going to stick.'

Conner began dribbling hot coffee around the room, soiling the cream carpet.

'Don't go thinking this is over, bitch. I'll be back, and you're going to tell me everything I need to know. Underestimate me at your peril. You've got forty-eight hours from now.'

Chapter 28

Tom stood staring at the carpet, a confused look of exasperation obvious on his face.

'What on earth happened here?'

'I spent about two hours trying to clean the damn thing,' Anna muttered. 'It's a lost cause. It's ruined. And we haven't even finished paying for it yet. Maybe we can claim on the insurance.'

Tom hugged her with a mix of affection and concern.

'It's not the end of the world. It's just a carpet at the end of the day, not flesh and blood. But, how on earth…? Did you have some sort of accident?'

Anna froze, her chest tightening, a pain in the back of her throat.

'I'm so very sorry, Tom. There's something we need to talk about. I really don't know where I'm going to start.'

He released his grip, the mood changing.

'You haven't met somebody else, have you?'

'No, no, of *course* not, it's nothing like that. Don't be so ridiculous.'

'Please don't tell me you're ill? I know the stress has been getting to you. I've told you to take it easy. I said—'

'Please stop, Tom, it's not about me, or at least not directly. We need to talk about my sister.'

'Kathy? Oh God, they haven't found her body, have they?'

Anna shook her head. 'Sit down, Tom, and please try to be understanding. I was just doing my best in difficult circumstances. I need you to understand that.'

Tom lowered himself into the nearest armchair, perching on the edge.

'Just say it, Anna, no secrets. You know I'm here for you. Whatever the situation, we'll deal with it like we always do.'

'Mike was here this morning. The bullying bastard! He arrived seconds after you left. I think he must have watched you go before hammering on the door.'

'I noticed a police car in the street, but I didn't think.'

'Yeah, that must have been him.'

'What did he want?'

'Um, he… eh… he demanded to know where Kathy is.'

'Kathy? But that suggests he didn't kill her?'

'He, er, he didn't, Kathy's not dead. The blood, the other evidence, it was all a sham. She's alive and well and living a few miles from Caerystwyth, a small town in West Wales. She's even got a job working part-time in a local veggie place. I received an email a couple of days back asking me to visit. I should have told you before. I really wish I had now.'

Tom loosened his collar.

'I *knew* there was something you weren't telling me. You and Kathy have always been so close. You weren't nearly upset enough to be mourning her death. Why on *earth* did you keep it from me? I've never given you any reason not to trust me. Not even once.'

'I'm sorry, Kathy made me promise. I thought I was doing the right thing.'

'Did you tell him… Mike – did you tell him?'

Anna pointed to the floor.

'What do you think?'

'He did that?'

'Oh yeah, and he made all sorts of threats. He scared me, Tom. God knows what it must have been like living with the man. I was crapping myself the entire time he was here. But I didn't tell him a damned thing.'

'I'd like to punch him in the mouth.'

She smiled.

'We've just got to hold our nerve, that's all. I don't care how many threats he makes. If he ever finds Kathy, it won't be because of anything I've said. I can't imagine what he'd do to her, but it wouldn't be good.'

'You've gone this far. There's no going back now. I just wish you'd trusted me.'

Kathy nodded. 'Yeah, I should have. I know that now.'

'Are you going to visit Kathy, like she asked?'

Anna fussed with her sleeve.

'I was thinking of booking a day off next Friday, if that's okay with you. I'd drive back on the Sunday for work the next day.'

'Do you want me to come with you? I'd be happy to if you'd like the company.'

Anna hesitated before replying.

'Um, I think it may be better if I go alone the first time. Telling you was never part of the plan. I'd like to explain everything to Kathy face-to-face, just the two of us. It's a twin thing. I don't want her thinking I've let her down.'

'If you're sure?'

Anna nodded.

'Yeah, I know it's for the best. We can visit together once Kathy knows what's happening, perhaps in the summer.'

He rose to his feet.

'Fancy a cup of tea? I'm off coffee for some reason.'

She smiled despite the tension. 'Tea would be lovely. Thanks for not giving me a hard time. It's been a tough few months. You're a wonderful partner, Tom. I appreciate your kindness.'

Conner held his smartphone just a few inches from his face, listening to the entirety of Anna and Tom's conversation for the third time in a little over an hour. So, the bitch was still alive and well. Just as he'd suspected. Just as he'd known all along.

He pictured Kathy's trembling image and addressed her in clear unambiguous tones, as if she were next to him.

'I'm coming after you, you disloyal, holier-than-thou bitch. I'm going to tear you apart. I'll bite your fucking face off!'

He slumped back in his seat, fatigued, panting, but also aroused. Follow Anna to Wales. That's all he had to do. It was just a matter of days. He'd get his hands on Kathy. He just had to be patient. Bide his time.

'Make the most of your sad life while you can, little Kathy Conner. I'm coming after you. Count the seconds, bitch. It will all be over soon.'

Chapter 29

Conner was glad of the cloud cover as he left his blood-soaked house at two forty-five the following morning. He drove cautiously, keen to avoid bringing any attention to his convertible as he implemented the next stage of his plan. He parked in a predictably quiet residential street following an uneventful journey, a rapid ten-minute walk away from Anna and Tom's modest but comfortable home.

Conner walked in the shadows, collar up, face focussed on the pavement as he approached Anna's car. It only took him a matter of minutes to open the driver's door, utilising a technique popular with local criminals. He reached down, sliding back the seat to maximum before fixing a fully charged battery-powered GPS tracking device below it, securing the unit in place with a length of double-sided black velcro tape. He switched on his phone, tapped on the tracking unit's accompanying software, waited a few seconds and then smiled upon confirming everything was in working order.

Conner slid the seat back to its original position, exited the vehicle, closed the door carefully and then headed back towards his car with a growing sense of achievement that bordered on the orgasmic. Everything was in place. On his laptop, on his phone. The final pieces of the jigsaw. And his ultimate triumph was fast approaching. He could almost touch it. Could almost smell Kathy's terror in the air and taste it on his breath.

He started the convertible's powerful engine, humming along to its mechanical growl as he negotiated the first bend at speed, having abandoned all thoughts of caution. Just days to go, just days, just days!

'I'm coming for you, Kathy, I'm coming. And there's nothing you can do to stop me.'

Chapter 30

Conner stared at his magnified phone screen, tracking Anna's car in real time as she drove out of Plymouth towards the M5 motorway and the M4 beyond. He'd begun his journey as she approached the outskirts of the city, pressing his foot down on the accelerator when busy traffic flow allowed; keen to stay within half a mile or so of his target prey. Conner screamed with frustration when delayed behind a stationary removal lorry, but he relaxed almost immediately as the road cleared in front of him. As he drove in the direction of Bristol, his anticipation engendered a range of familiar feelings and emotions that bordered on ecstasy. He could feel Kathy's neck in his hands as he squeezed the steering wheel tighter. He could hear her visceral screams soaring like a classical aria that drowned out his thinking and sent hormones surging through his body.

Time seemed to be passing slowly when Conner checked the time as he paid the toll in cash to cross the suspension bridge spanning the Severn Estuary. Anna had stopped at two service stations en route, once to purchase petrol at a seemingly inflated price, and once to sit and drink sweet coffee as she read a discarded broadsheet paper. Conner briefly considered approaching her, demanding answers, more as a result of frustration than reasoned thought, but he abandoned the idea at the last second, retreating to his car where he waited for her to continue her journey west.

Conner watched as Anna drove back in the direction of the M4, allowing the hatchback to leave his sight before following at a distance he considered best negated the possibility of detection. Within the hour he was approaching the faded industrial town of

Llanelli, with Anna just a few miles ahead. He envisaged finding Kathy that very day. Picturing the glorious climax to his plan of revenge. But as he pulled into the outside lane, his car suddenly swerved. A rear tyre deflating as a three-inch nail penetrated the worn rubber. Conner's convertible hit the central safety barrier with force, spinning and narrowly avoiding several other vehicles as their drivers either hit their breaks or manoeuvred past at speed. Conner lost consciousness as his head cracked the windscreen, the car coming to an eventual halt on the hard shoulder, with scalding vapour erupting from the fractured radiator and spiralling into the winter air.

It was already dark by the time Conner woke in West Wales General Hospital. His head pounded as he sat up in his acute admissions bed, waving frantically to the nearest sky-blue uniformed staff nurse, who approached with a look of resigned acceptance.

'It's nice to see you awake. You've been out of it for almost four hours. How's your forehead feeling? You had quite a bang.'

Conner raised a hand to his face.

'My phone, where the hell's my phone?'

'You didn't have it on you when you arrived.'

'Oh, for fucks sake! What about my wallet?'

She smiled nervously.

'I put it in the safe.'

'Where the hell am I?'

'You don't know?'

He felt his muscles bunch.

'Just answer the fucking question, woman. I asked, didn't I?'

She tensed.

'You're in West Wales General.'

'How far's that from Caerystwyth?'

'We're on the outskirts of town. Five minutes by car or a fifteen-minute walk.'

Conner looked himself up and down.

'Have I broken anything?'

'No, but the consultant says you're concussed. You need to lie down and relax. Shall I get you a glass of water?'

'What's this thing in my arm?'

'It's saline. It's nothing to worry about.'

'Get it out!'

'Please try to relax, sir. I'll fetch a doctor.'

He tore the micropore from his arm before pulling out the tube with a pained whelp.

'My wallet, where the fuck's my wallet?'

An older and more senior nurse arrived at his bedside.

'Please settle down, Mr Conner, your wallet is perfectly safe. Try to behave yourself. This is a hospital ward, not a playground.'

Conner bared his teeth, bawling with an animalistic snarl.

'Just get the fucking thing and that's an instruction, not a request.'

'Please try to settle down, sir, or I'll have to contact the police.'

He jumped from the bed, rushing towards her, yelling in her face.

'I *am* the fucking police! Now, get my wallet like I told you to. Now, woman, I'm out of here. There's things I need to do, important things. There's not a second to waste.'

Chapter 31

Conner had thrown up twice by the time he found Caerystwyth's only three-star hotel in a built-up street on the outskirts of town. He staggered into the comfortably furnished reception with a credit card in hand, booking a one-night stay before stumbling into the lift, his pounding headache causing him to curse crudely as he searched for his second-floor room. He slumped onto the king-size bed, fully intending to take a quick nap – but within minutes fell into a deep sleep that lasted hours.

Conner woke with a start, leaping from bed, throwing open the curtains and staring out on the town as the day's light faded. He checked the time, rushing towards the bathroom to empty his bladder on realising it was already late afternoon. He splashed cold water on his face in an attempt to focus. He was in Wales for a reason. For revenge. It was time to make it happen. There was no more time to rest.

Within minutes Conner was back in reception, standing at the counter with his elbows resting on top.

'What day is it?'

The young woman took a backward step.

'Saturday, it's Saturday.'

'Saturday afternoon?'

'Yes, that's right, Saturday afternoon.'

'How many vegetarian eateries are there here in town?'

She chewed at her bottom lip, avoiding eye contact. 'Are you okay, sir? Is there anything I can get you? You don't seem at all well.'

'Just answer the fucking question.'

She rushed her reply. 'There's three, just three.'

'Where exactly?'

'One's opposite the market in Curzon Street, there's one close to the park, I don't know the name of the street, and there's one in Merlin's Lane.'

'Which is nearest?'

'Um, the one by the park. It's on the opposite side of the road near the main entrance. You can't miss it.'

'How far?'

'A ten-minute walk at most. But I can order you a taxi if that helps?'

Conner turned without response, shoving open the glass doors. His mind was focussed on only one thing. Kathy's time had come.

Chapter 32

Kathy served Anna with her third cup of coffee with a smile.

'Are you sure you don't mind hanging around until I finish? I should be done by soon after six. And it's all in a good cause. We're raising money for a Parkinson's charity.'

Anna shook her head.

'I don't mind at all. I've got my coffee, a cake and a good book. I'm just happy to spend some time with you. It's great to see you looking so happy.'

Kathy beamed.

'I can't believe how much life has changed in such a short time. I've got you to thank of that.'

'Oh, come on, you did most of it yourself, Kathy. Don't sell yourself short. You should be very proud of yourself.'

'Well, I'm grateful – and I always will be.' And then she whispered, barely audible. 'Please call me Hazel while you're here. I should have said something before.'

Anna nodded without words.

'Thank you, Anna.'

Anna reached for her handbag.

'I'm going to head outside for a fag, *Hazel*.'

'Don't tell me you've started smoking again?'

Anna frowned.

'Yeah, I hadn't touched the damned things for years. It's the stress. Or at least that's my excuse. I'll give up again before heading home. Tom would be horrified. He can't stand the smell.'

'I'm not going to lecture you. You know they're bad news. That's why you gave up in the first place.'

Anna stood.

'Do you mind if I borrow your coat? It's frigging freezing out there.'

'Help yourself, it's on the back of the door.'

Anna slipped it on, fastening the buttons.

'You've had this for years.'

'Dad bought it as a birthday gift before I met Mike. Do you remember? I hid it from Mike at the bottom of a wardrobe. He'd never have let me keep it.'

Anna laughed, focussing on the good, choosing to forget the bad.

'Dad gave me a bright orange one with the same style. I always preferred yours. I don't think I ever wore mine.'

Kathy laughed at the memory as her twin approached the door.

'I'll see you in five minutes, Anna. I'd better get back to work. We can talk more later. We've got all the time in the world.'

Chapter 33

Conner spotted the woman wearing the familiar scarlet coat almost as soon as he hurried into Merlin's Lane at just gone five that evening. She was sitting, huddled on a low wall bordering an unlit area of rough grass, just off the main thoroughfare. Conner noticed that the woman was smoking as he crept towards her; blowing clouds of toxic fumes around her head. He thought it odd initially, but it didn't faze him for very long. Her hair was different. She'd dyed it again. But it was Kathy, all right. He'd recognise the moronic cow anywhere. Little Kathy Conner in all her faded glory. Blowing smoke into the starlit sky. What a bitch! It seemed she was capable of almost anything.

Anna was oblivious to Conner's presence as he picked a discarded beer bottle from the ground and slowly approached her. By the time she finally heard his footfalls and turned to face him, it was already too late. Conner lifted the heavy brown bottle high above his head and brought it crashing down, once, then again, fatally fracturing Anna's skull long before she fell and hit the ground. He stood over her, repeating the process, raining down blow after blow until Anna's face was an unrecognisable bloody pulp. Conner froze momentarily as a man yelled out somewhere in the distance, but he quickly regained his composure, smashing the bottle to the ground and starting to run as Anna's unseeing eyes stared into the unseen distance.

Kathy opened the cafe door just in time to see her husband sprint past, covered in blood from head to foot. She saw him clearly, but he didn't see her as he increased his pace. Two local men were chasing him now, as Anna lay dead. Conner was looking ahead. Focussed on escape. His ability for reasoned thought severely

191

impaired by his growing sense of indignation. Kathy was dead! The bitch was dead. And that was no more than she deserved. Why were the bastards chasing him? Why couldn't the chasers understand his behaviour? His actions were reasonable, weren't they? Yes, entirely reasonable! Kathy had brought everything on herself. It was her fault, not his. Just like before.

Kathy watched from a distance as Conner was wrestled to the ground. When she first noticed Anna, her mouth dropped open in shock. She ran towards her, immediately performing CPR, and kept going until she gave up six minutes later. Kathy sat on the hard, cold ground, exhausted and wailing as Conner was dragged away by two uniformed officers who had arrived on the scene. Maybe it really was over. Surely not even he could escape justice this time.

Kathy picked up Anna's handbag, checked for her car keys, and began walking away with a deluge of warm tears streaming down her face, as the gathering crowd looked on. If only Anna hadn't visited. If only she'd stayed away. Conner was a monster. What the hell was wrong with the man? He'd brought nothing but suffering and misery into the world. She really should have killed him when she had the chance. Stupid girl! She admonished herself time and again. It was her fault, her fault. If she'd killed the bastard Anna would still be alive.

Chapter 34

Kathy sang along to an early Roberta Flack CD, making no effort to hold back the tears as she drove in the direction of Caerystwyth Police Station on the outskirts of town. She cursed loudly as she crunched the gears for a second time. Fuck it! One more failure to drag her down. She hadn't driven for years. She was out of practice. Finding Anna's car had been easy enough in the end. But maybe driving it wasn't such a good idea after all.

Kathy pulled up at the side of the road as her grief beat her down a little further, coming in waves with no room for denial. She screamed at the top of her voice, loud, visceral. She pounded the steering wheel with the sides of clenched fists as she pictured Anna lying on the cold ground, her head caved in, dark blood pouring from her wounds. It was an image she knew she'd never forget. A picture she could never erase from her mind for however long she lived. It would always be there as if in real time. A vivid reminder of her greatest sorrow.

Kathy raised a hand to her face. Anna, poor Anna! Her sister was dead in her place. Who'd have thought it? There was no justice in the world. Anna had done nothing but help. She'd shown her nothing but kindness. What did Anna do to deserve her fate? Kathy pictured her husband's mocking face and hated him more than she'd ever thought possible. She felt as if a limb had been ripped from her body. As if a part of her was dead. And in a way it was. They'd been two sides of the same coin. Two sisters who shared so much.

Kathy blinked away her tears as a rainbow appeared before her. A bright arc of spectral colours, red, orange, yellow, green, blue, indigo, and violet, that became visible in the sky opposite the winter sun as tiny drops of misty rain began to fall. She looked out on the grand vista and smiled through her tears, interpreting its beauty as a sign intended for her and only her. Her sister was in a better place. Of course, she was. A safer place where she knew nothing but love. And Anna wanted the best for her too. That seemed obvious. She approved of her intended actions. She knew they made sense. What other explanation was there? She had to stay safe. The baby had to stay safe. And she had to do whatever it took to secure that end. All doubts were suddenly gone. Kathy knew what she had to do. And Anna understood that. That's what Kathy told herself. That's what she repeated in her mind. The rainbow was getting brighter. It was, wasn't it? Kathy craned her neck towards the windscreen and stared. Yes, yes, it was, it definitely was. Anna was in full agreement. Just do it, Kathy. Stay safe, girl. Forget convention. Forget the rules. She'd got this far by using her initiative. Whatever it takes.

Kathy restarted the engine and continued her journey in the certain knowledge that she was doing the correct thing. A small but vocal part of her still wanted to retreat back to her remote caravan sanctuary, but what would that achieve? The bastard wouldn't be in prison forever, however long his sentence. He'd serve fifteen maybe twenty years at most. One day he'd be back on the streets and full of hateful intentions. Focussed on revenge if such a thing were possible. He'd come after her if he had even the slightest opportunity. Kathy knew that with every cell of her being. He'd never let it go. She'd never been more certain of anything in her life. There was only one option left open to her. Circumstances offered an opportunity. She had to disappear once and for all.

Kathy switched on the car's headlights as the sky darkened and the rain became heavier, large drops of cold water bouncing off the road as the wipers fought to clear her view. Come on, Kathy, keep going. You can do it, girl. It was time to do what she had to do. Time to get it over with. Time to take control.

Kathy pressed her foot down on the accelerator and increased her pace. Within ten minutes or so West Wales Police Headquarters came into view through a thin mist that had swept in off the sea. Kathy pulled off the road and into the busy car park, finding a free space just as the final song reached a dramatic crescendo before the CD came to a timely end. She switched off the engine and sat there for a few seconds attempting to calm her racing mind. This was it. The time had come. There was no going back now. Not if she wanted a better life. She had to be convincing. It had to be the best acting performance of her life.

Kathy exited the car and walked slowly towards the main entrance, strangely oblivious to the driving rain as it soaked her to the skin and chilled her to the bone. She stopped momentarily on reaching the door, urging herself on as she opened it and stepped into the warmth to be met by a friendly receptionist who looked up and smiled to greet her.

'How can help you?'

Kathy swallowed hard, swaying from one foot to the other. 'My name's Anna Oakes. I'm here to see a Detective Inspector Laura Kesey. She's heading up my sister's murder investigation. I need to make a statement. My brother-in-law did it. He's in custody. He's one vicious bastard. I saw everything that happened.'

Chapter 35

The journey from West Wales to Plymouth passed more quickly than Kathy would have wished in a perfect world. She'd convinced the Welsh police of her new identity easily enough, but there were more significant challenges ahead. Kathy parked her sister's hatchback almost directly outside the Oakes' terraced home, exiting the car with a thin smile on her face, to be met by Tom who was already waiting in the open doorway. He stepped out into the cold, throwing his arms around her and pulling her close.

'It's lovely to see you, Anna.'

'You too, I've been counting the minutes.'

'Your hair looks different.'

Kathy's gut twisted.

'Yes, I had it done on the morning of the murder. It seems so utterly unimportant now, but I fancied a change at the time. I'd like to think Kathy would approve.'

'I'm so very sorry about Kathy, Anna. But at least Mike's been caught and locked up, that's some consolation. I hope the vicious bastard never sees the light of day again.'

'He won't if I've got anything to do with it.'

Tom led Kathy into the hallway, holding her hand tightly in his.

'It was awful, Tom. I actually saw Mike running away from the crime scene covered in Kathy's blood. The murder weapon was on the ground next to her body. I tried to save her. I really did! But it was already too late. Her injuries were horrendous. She never stood a chance.'

'I know love, I know. You did everything you could.'

Kathy slumped onto the sofa, her eyes bright as she looked up at him.

'There's going to be a post-mortem before the funeral. There's no avoiding it, apparently. Or at least that's what the Welsh police said.'

'I guess that's inevitable given the circumstances.'

'It seems so.'

'Does your mother know?'

'I haven't talked to her as yet. I'm trying not to think about it. A part of me would prefer not to talk to her at all.'

'You can't put it off forever.'

'I know. Believe me, I know. Sit down, Tom. There's something I haven't told you.'

His breathing accelerated as he sat alongside her. 'Oh God, what now?'

It was now or never. 'No, you can relax, it's good news. Or at least I think it's good. I hope you agree.'

'Okay, I'm listening.'

'We're going to have a baby.'

Tom's mouth fell open.

'What? You're pregnant? But I thought we couldn't…'

'Doctors aren't always right. This is our little miracle.'

'Oh, that is absolutely fantastic! I'd almost given up on it ever happening.' He studied her closely. 'Wow, I can see the slight bump now you've told me. I can't believe I didn't notice anything before.'

'It's only just started showing. You must have noticed I've been wearing baggy jumpers.'

He hadn't noticed a thing. 'Um, yeah, I guess so, now that you mention it.'

'I'm so glad you're pleased.'

He moved up close.

'How far gone are you? When did you find out?'

'I'm about sixteen weeks. I wanted to make sure everything was okay before telling you. There was so much going on. I've been worried that something was going to go horribly wrong.'

Tom decided to let it slide.

'If it's a girl we should name her after your sister.'

Kathy wiped a tear from her face.

'I think that's a lovely idea. Kathy would be so very proud.'

'How about a nice cup of coffee to celebrate the pregnancy?'

'Tea for me, please.' Kathy patted her stomach. 'Needs must and all that. Shall I make it?'

'No, you stay there and rest. You need looking after. You've had a long day.'

Tom handed Kathy a pottery mug filled almost to the brim.

'There you go, Anna. There's a piece of cake on the way.'

'I'd prefer toast.'

'Really?'

'Please.'

Kathy sipped her tea, grimacing.

'Oh, too sweet!'

He looked down at her with a quizzical expression.

'But I only added two teaspoonfuls, the same as usual.'

'Maybe it's a pregnancy thing.'

'I guess it must be.'

Kathy closed her eyes for a beat before opening them again and staring at the ceiling.

'I've changed, Tom. Kathy's death tore me in two. I'm not the woman you married anymore. You'll have to be patient with me and particularly until the trial's over. I need you to understand that.'

He studied her familiar features, asking himself questions he didn't want to answer.

'Of *course*, I understand. It's going to be tough on you, but we'll get through it together. We'll do *whatever* it takes. Nothing is more important. We're going to be a family now. I want that more than anything.'

Made in the USA
Columbia, SC
18 June 2019

But after Sheila's decades-old secret comes to the surface, she has to decide if righting a wrong from her past is worth destroying her future. Can Sheila and Russell find a way through, or is their second chance at happiness too good to be true?

Pre-order your copy today and get ready for another heartwarming series on San Juan Island!

Would you like to join my reader group?

Sign up for my reader newsletter and get a free copy of my novella Christmas at Saltwater Cove. You can sign up by visiting: https://bit.ly/XmasSWC

About the Author

Amelia Addler writes always sweet, always swoon-worthy romance stories and believes that everyone deserves their own happily ever after.

Her soulmate is a man who once spent five weeks driving her to work at 4AM after her car broke down (and he didn't complain, not even once). She is lucky enough to be married to that man and they live in Pittsburgh with their little yellow mutt. Visit her website at AmeliaAddler.com or drop her an email at amelia@AmeliaAddler.com.

Also by Amelia...

The Spotted Cottage Series
The Spotted Cottage by the Sea

The Westcott Bay Series
Saltwater Cove

Saltwater Studios

Saltwater Secrets

Saltwater Crossing

Saltwater Falls

Saltwater Memories

Saltwater Promises

Christmas at Saltwater Cove

The Orcas Island Series
Sunset Cove

Sunset Secrets

Sunset Tides

Sunset Weddings

Sunset Serenade